A New Dance

By Kara S. McKenzie

Acknowledgements

I want to thank both my family and friends in their continued support of my book. I cannot name all of those who encouraged me in so many different ways, by reading my books, giving suggestions and helping me realize my potential. Those included are my immediate family, my extended family, my Bible study group, my school friends, my on-line writer buddies, and both my Cedarville, Climax and Scott's hometown friends. I truly appreciate all the loving support shown.

Dedication

To my family and friends.

A New Dance

By Kara S. McKenzie

"In those days there was no king in Israel: every man did that which was right in his own eyes." Judges 21:25 King James's Version

Chapter 1

Mara turned to her daughter, who was sitting beside her on stone steps leading to the doorway of their home. "You need to be careful, child. You should stay close to us." The older woman looked out past the courtyard and down the dusty rock-strewn road. It was as though she were contemplating a storm approaching in the distance, with her grim expression and furrowed brow.

Keturah smiled while holding her scarf about her head, eying the path in front of the house. She shook her head. She'd spent so much of her childhood in her parent's protective care, yet they needed to begin trusting her to make her own decisions. "Mother, seventeen's hardly a child. I've been taking water from the well to fill the cistern since I was very young, and of course I'll be with Betsalel." Keturah lifted her gaze to the hills beyond their home. "Besides, nothing ever happens in Shiloh, with our city so centrally located in Israel."

She brushed off the new tunic her mother made her out of spun and dyed flax. The fabric was a lovely color of lilacs, gathered from a myrtle plant not far from their home. Tirzah would love it. She couldn't wait for her friend to see it.

Again, she looked out past the stone gate of the courtyard and down the path in front of their home. Gritty sand blew in wisps over the tops of the courtyard wall. Swirling and spinning particles disappeared on the ground as they landed on the other side.

Keturah's mother pounded bread dough in a wooden bowl, as she sat on the stone steps at the doorway to the house. The tap, tapping sound clicked against the side of it in a patterned rhythm. She looked up at Keturah with questioning eyes.

Keturah smiled. She loved her parents dearly, but it was easier when she was a child.

She remembered going out in the hills near her home barefoot, letting the leather cords out of her hair, dancing and turning in circles, tumbling to the ground and not worrying about dangers or what she'd look like to others. Afterward, she'd lie there and look up at the expanse of the sky, knowing she never wanted to leave Shiloh, ever.

But, because she was a woman now, her parent's had different expectations, and it wasn't the same. She'd learned to be the quiet contemplative, obedient daughter they wished her to be, going about her tasks at home and staying close to family, rather than that young girl, unhindered by rules and propriety.

She let out a breath. Where was Tirzah?

Goats bleated quietly in the fields nearby, while a shepherd man with badly worn fur coverings, staff in hand, led a flock of sheep to a pasture further away.

Keturah tipped her head, watching him, waiting for her friend. She lifted her face to the sun, relishing the cool morning air. The breeze was light. It was a good day to walk.

Her father leaned over a fur hide he was working on. "How long will you be?"

The smell of hide was so strong Keturah turned her face away. "How do I know, father?" Her brow creased, and she let out a light sound, her answer uncommonly abrupt. "How long is it to the well and back?"

Her brothers, Caleb and Asher, on mats next to her father, quietly carved tools for later use.

Caleb stopped a moment and looked up at her. "You should listen to father. And not speak to him like that." He gave her a stern tip of the head, and then looked back down at the flint-bladed sickle he held in his hand, chipping away at the point. He went back to work.

Keturah sighed. Her brother was right. She should've answered her father's question without complaint. Sometimes, she couldn't seem to quell the urge to reveal what was on her mind when she spoke to her parents. And yet, all her father had done is asked a simple question. He didn't deserve her harsh answer.

She turned. "Sorry, father. It shouldn't take long. Unless there are other women getting water too."

Her mother put the bowl down. She got up and went to Keturah, reaching out and smoothing back the dark curls that floated freely down her daughter's back. "You're a good girl. But, you're wrong. There's always plenty of trouble in the city and some areas you shouldn't ever go to. The people don't listen to our Lord anymore and go their own way. If anything should ever happen to you, it would be hard on your father and I. And a little black goat isn't what I'd call protection. Betsalel will not help in these situations, and you know it."

She lifted a swatch of cream-colored fabric from her pile of cloth and wrapped it around Keturah's shoulders.

Keturah couldn't help smiling. Her mother was right about the goat, and yet Shiloh was tame in her eyes. Little had ever happened there, and she wasn't afraid. She didn't plan on going far. "I'm sorry, mother, but Tirzah's meeting me. We're taking the paths to the well together."

Keturah looked out past the gate. "There." She pointed down the path. "Look!" She called to her friend. "Tirzah! You've come!"

A young woman with straight black hair swinging freely over her shoulder made her way toward them, standing at the end of the walk holding a water jar and waving.

"Keturah!" Tirzah's eyes were dancing.

Caleb and Asher both looked up from what they were doing and watched Keturah's friend.

Keturah smiled at the way people took notice of Tirzah. The young woman drew others to her like a pasture to sheep. There were few times when her friend wasn't laughing about something or teasing those around her in a good-natured way. And in addition to her high-spirited antics, no one could deny that her beauty was both inside and out. Her sparkling, brown eyes shone, as she smiled with rows of straight teeth, and her dark skin complemented every tunic she wore. There wasn't a man alive in the village able to keep their eyes off her when she walked past.

Keturah bolted out the heavy stone gate of their courtyard and called to Tirzah again. Then, she turned back to wave at her mother and father, who watched from behind. She picked up a clay water jar next to the gate and lifted it to her shoulder, while Betsalel tottered behind them. How fun it was to take the paths! The well wasn't far, but the women who came to it, often brought news of the city and beyond.

Tirzah stayed where she was, until Keturah reached her.

Her friend's dark, mischievous eyes were dancing. She pushed her braid behind her. "Ooh, a newly sewn tunic?" She let out a sweet sound of laughter. "It hugs your shape well."

"Tirzah, my parents will hear." Keturah's cheeks warmed. She looked back at her mother and father.

Tirzah laughed again, smoothing out her skirt. She had lowered her tone slightly, and yet her voice was still lively, as she fingered the soft, lavender fabric. And then, she let out a whistle. "It is surely pretty enough to turn heads. And I know who'll be looking too, every man in the village. I don't think you know how beautiful you are."

Keturah shook her head. "You think of the young men too often, I think." She smiled.

Tirzah held her fingers to her lips, as her eyes sparked to life again. "They say I've an eye for them."

Keturah laughed. "Oh, Tirzah. What am I to do with you?"

Tirzah snorted, smiling. "Ha! You know I'll never change. There is little you can do to remedy that."

Keturah grinned. She was right. No one ever told Tirzah what to do. She had a mind of her own and wasn't afraid to use it. Keturah often wondered what kind of man Tirzah would marry and whether or not he'd be as accepting of her fun-natured antics as her parents were.

"Come," Keturah replied. "Let's go see if there's any news from town. I'm sure we're bound to hear something at the well."

Both young women locked their free arms, as they made their way to one of the many wells in Shiloh. The air was cool as they strode down the hard, rocky path that ran between homes built of mud, and rounded stones that littered the path in town.

Keturah took a breath. Yellow wheat on one side of the road spread out like shimmering gold, the tops shivering and bending in the wind. Shiloh seemed to contain the breath of the Lord himself in its lovely fields.

Keturah's goat let out a sound and moved between her and Tirzah.

Tirzah looked down at the small animal.

Keturah reached out and tugged on his fur. "I'm sure he thinks I'm his mother." She cooed to the small black goat. "Come, Betsalel."

He lifted his ears to her voice and let out a sound.

Both girls smiled.

They neared the well. It was early morning.

Other women were already there, their brightly colored tunics and scarves dancing in the light wind, as they held onto their water jars waiting for their turn.

Keturah and Tirzah spoke quietly to each other while watching the others take the clear, cool liquid out of the well.

Keturah's eyes were drawn to the hillside in the distance. The sun was rising in the east behind them, sending a flood of colors over

4

the hill country of Ephraim. "It's so beautiful, here. I never want to leave it."

Tirzah sighed, nodding. "Yes, we'll marry men in Shiloh and raise our children here. And always be friends."

A sigh escaped Keturah, as orange-gold rays spread warmth over the meadows below. She leaned close to Tirzah and whispered in her ear. "Hiram and father are talking, very soon."

Tirzah bellowed, "About the engagement?" Her eyes were large.

Keturah put her fingers to her lips. She felt heat rush to her face. "Tirzah. Shush! Don't say it so loud."

Then Tirzah tipped her head to the side. She rested her hands in her lap. "Is it what you want?"

Keturah spoke in a hushed tone. "I'd be honored to have such hard-working, honest man. And if father and mother approve, I'm sure it'll be a good match."

Tirzah put her water jar down next to her. "It would secure a home here for you." She picked her container back up when it was their turn at the well.

They pulled on the ropes to draw the water out of the small hole at the top and then filled their jars and set them on their shoulders to take back to their homes.

On the way back, Tirzah was unusually silent. Her sandals tread softly over the path, but every now and then she would scrape the ground with the edge of her leathery sole.

The wind died slightly, and the meadow grasses seemed to stand at attention, waiting for the next breeze. Keturah suddenly stopped on the path. Tirzah was rarely at a loss for words. Keturah sensed her friend's pensive mood. "You've something on your mind?"

Tirzah sighed. She stared at the meadow, and then looked back at Keturah. "My friend, what if after your marriage, you realize you don't love him? Do you wonder whether or not you'll have feelings for him?"

Keturah shrugged, not quite understanding the question. "I suppose I never gave it much thought. He comes from a good family, and I know my parents approve in the end, so it's what matters most."

Tirzah's dark eyes slanted downward. "I suppose." She set the water jar on the ground and stood up. "But, I sure hope when I marry, it'll be like our patriarch, Caleb, having the great love he and Rachel had. It'd be what I'd wish for. They both seemed to know they loved each other as soon as they met."

Keturah smiled. "Hmm. But, remember Tirzah, they trusted the Lord to give them what he saw best. He can and will. Maybe we should worry about getting water for our cisterns instead, and let the Lord do his work. We mustn't let our emotions tell us the way to go."

The goat let out a bleating sound.

Keturah turned around and got down next to the small animal, petting the top of its head. She suddenly giggled. "But, if I do find Hiram less than what I expect, at least I'll have my goat and my place in Shiloh."

Tirzah laughed. "Hah! A fine consolation if you don't like the man."

Keturah laughed with her, and then stood back up and began walking again next to Tirzah's side.

They spoke little about the engagement after that, instead turning their thoughts to the news in the city, making their way down the path. It wasn't long before they parted ways to their homes.

*****

"Honour thy father and mother: that thy days may be long upon the land, which the Lord thy God giveth thee." Exodus 20:12 King James's Version

Chapter 2

Joash reached out and took a piece of dark bread off a platter and shoved it in his mouth, chewing unceremoniously. His dark green eyes glittered as he looked around the low table in his parent's candlelit room. A guest of his father was there with his two daughters who sat on mats at the end of the wooden table. The young women giggled and whispered, casting shy glances his way as they ate. It was obvious they were enamored with the idea of an arrangement made regarding him.

He ignored the young women, knowing full well his mother set all this up. He was determined anyone he took to his home in Bethel to be his wife, would be his sole choice and not part of any plan of his mother's. Besides, he had no interest in these girls who trained their eyes on him like prized livestock. And he wasn't sure he had time for any woman for that matter, at least not anytime soon.

He eyed the spread his mother had prepared. At least her meal was good. Baskets contained figs from the tree outside the home, and warm bread sat on a platter in the middle of the table with oil for dipping it in. Another oblong-shaped wooden bowl was piled high with meat from a lamb recently butchered, along with a block of goat cheese.

"Joash." His father gestured to their guests. "This is Dinah and Tamara. They're my friend's girls and have come a distance to see us, all the way from Shiloh to north of us. They're Ephraimites."

Joash nodded dutifully. "It's good to meet you." He lifted one brow, cramming another piece of bread in his mouth as he spoke, hoping to hold them at bay with his less than considerate manners.

Both girls giggled, ignoring his behavior. They looked down at their plates and then back up, smiling as if they hadn't noticed.

He shrugged, looking back at the food.

His mother had placed a large bowl of pottage in the center of the table and ladled some of the thick broth into bowls for them. She gave him a stern look.

He dipped the bread into it and scooped the whole thing into his mouth. "Thank you, mother. It's good as usual." He gave her a heartwarming grin.

She shook her head and pursed her lips, not responding.

He let out a grunt, chuckling to himself. She wanted so much to see him married and settled. He hadn't given much thought to it, but knew when the time came he'd take care of the matter himself. At the moment, he considered women more trouble than they were worth.

His mother ladled out a small amount for his sister, Nissa, who was seated beside him.

He scowled at the way his sister meekly accepted her serving. Her eyes were downcast.

Her muteness was annoying. He was sure she could talk, but purposely chose not to. She obviously understood everything said to her, because of the way she followed directions, when given. Their parent's needed to stop coddling her, because without speech, what good would she be to anyone? It wouldn't be long and she'd be old enough to leave the home.

He listened to the conversation at the table, avoiding eye contact with the women across from him, while he finished his meal. He tapped his fingers impatiently on the table, as the others spoke for what seemed like hours.

One of the young women fingered a strand of hair and looked up at him, her lips slightly open.

He lifted a brow at the obvious intention in her eyes.

He laughed to himself. This woman had no understanding of what she'd be getting herself into, making ties with a man like him. If she thought he was anything like his father, she couldn't have been more wrong. After spending the years as he had in the company he kept, he had little clue how to treat a woman, at least the way they'd want him to.

He pushed the dark hair that hung over his forehead back and smiled again guardedly, getting up from the table. "I don't mean to be impolite, but there are a few things I need to be doing."

"You don't need to go just yet, son." His father stood and patted Joash on the shoulder.

"I've tasks at hand."

His father nodded. "My son's skilled with the sling, one of the famous left-handers of the tribe, a true Benjamite. He's one of the strongest soldiers, and as you can see very tall."

8

Joash turned, his mouth curving upward. He grabbed a fur mantle from a stand next to him and lifted it over his shoulders. Then, he tipped his head to both the girls and their father. "I hope you'll enjoy the rest of the meal and that you'll have a safe journey back."

Both girls returned his nod, lowering their heads, their eyes shining.

He shoved the door open and didn't look back, eager to get outside where he could wash his hands of his mother's schemes.

His father gave him a look that made it clear they'd talk later.

Joash turned and stooped to get through the doorway and into the courtyard.

Once outside, he sucked in some air, sighing with relief. He'd go back for more of his mother's pottage later. It was too stifling in that tiny room to eat any more. And besides, he needed to get some work done.

He grabbed his sling and bow from inside another room and strode purposefully through the gate of the courtyard and to the stable built into the side of a rocky wall near their home. He quickly mounted his horse, making his way out of the gate to the outskirts of the city of Bethel and into the grassy plains.

His parent's plans would have to wait.

***

"Joash isn't listening to us." Mary let out a breath. "Simeon, you have to talk to him. He doesn't understand the importance of the decisions he's making and won't heed what I say."

Simeon shook his head. "Mary, please. You know how hard I've tried. And also how mule-headed he can be? He doesn't want a wife."

The lines in Mary's face deepened. She was obviously not consoled by her husband's answer. "It isn't that he hasn't had the chance. Most every woman in the village has had their heart set on him. He's strong and capable and would be a good provider. And no one denies the fact that he is considered one of the finest of his regiment in Gibeah. He could easily have any of them."

"Maybe. But, if they're not the choice the Lord wishes for him, it wouldn't be a good match." Simeon's eyes softened. "Remember, the more you push, the more Joash seems to resent the idea. He doesn't need your interference."

He put his hand gently on her shoulder. "We must remember that the Lord has a plan, one better for Joash than anything we might want. You must leave it in the Lord's hands and not try to impose your will in it. "

Mary let out a sigh. "I wish I could. But, it's not so easy to do. Especially when hope for it seems to be fading. There should be grandchildren. It's our heritage and legacy to keep the tribe strong and pass on the Benjamite name. And Joash knows this."

"But, Mary, remember. The Lord can do what we can't. Where's your faith?" Simeon challenged her.

Mary rubbed her temples. "But, I've waited on the Lord and prayed, and time seems to be at a standstill. Joash isn't getting any younger. Nothing's as easy as it seems."

Simeon smiled, taking her hand. "A mother's love is strong. But, do not be pained. The Lord knows you want what's best for him and will see you through."

"Oh Simeon. I'm sorry for the trouble I am. I will try to leave things alone, but can't promise anything. I want so much for him to find a wife, mostly so that he'll be settled and know what it is to love as we do."

Simeon squeezed her hand. "I know it's difficult for you. I will continue to pray and trust the Lord. We can count on him."

*****

"And it was so, that all that saw it said, There was no such deed done nor seen from the day that the children of Israel came up out of the land of Egypt unto this day…" Judges 19: 30 King James's Version

Chapter 3

While Mara baked bread in the courtyard, Keturah saw her chance. She left her weaving loom, and snuck out to find her way to the hillside with Betsalel. It was too lovely of a day for her to sit inside, as the sun was just peeking over the horizon.

The meadow was bright with flowers, and the countryside beyond the city flamed with colors. She looked out over the vast slopes of hills in the distance and let out a long, slow breath. In this place behind her house, the valley took a dip, and she could stand on the side of the hill unnoticed. She took the confining scarf from her head, letting her dark curls escape freely down her back and tipped her head to the sun.

She felt the soft warmth of the morning rays upon her skin and began to dance, turning to the sound of the bird's soft melodies and the whisper of the wind on the grass. Her movements were like floating leaves and fluid as the bend of a tree's limb.

She danced to the Lord, as Miriam of old, freeing herself to honor him, murmuring soft prayers from her lips in wild abandon, like she'd remembered doing as a child. The air entering her lungs felt fresh as heaven, and she relished the thought of the Lord watching, his eyes tender and full of love.

She danced contentedly under what seemed like a colored dome of heaven, while the fog rose and fell around her. It was as if she were in the clouds herself and was seeing the Father's breath.

After a time, she slowed her spins, staring at the sky, watching a dove spiral downward to the ground. She let out a sigh and clasped her hands behind her, willing nothing to disturb the tranquil feeling that swept through her.

She finally sat on the ground, while Betsalel, her shadow, came to nibble at her skirt. She tugged the cloth away, laughing. "Come, my little pet. You must get back to your pen and me to my cloth. Mother will find us soon, and then we'll be in trouble."

She tied her scarf back on and ruffled his head, getting up to walk back to the house. A sense of peace filled her inside, convincing her the Lord was close at hand.

***

Later on, Keturah sifted through soft fibers of goat's hair on a mat in the small courtyard of their mud brick home. It would dry fast in this place.

She looked out the arched entrance of stone. Her brother was making his way to the house. His mouth was grim and turned downward.

"What is it, Caleb?" She tugged on his robe, as he stepped over the uneven doorstep and into the cramped area where she sat. She stood up, questions racing through her mind. His lip was a thin line, and his jaw was clenched. "Brother?"

He didn't answer, as he shot past her.

She followed him up a narrow block staircase built alongside the inner wall that led to an upper chamber of their home. He waved her away from the small doorway at the top. "You don't want to hear this."

Keturah ducked inside the opening behind him, interested. Whatever happened, she could tell by the look on his face it wasn't good. "Tell me? Please, Caleb?"

He took quick strides straight to their father, who was kneeling on a woven mat next to an oil lamp at the table. His head was bent in prayer. The room was dark and flickered with the light from the flame.

It took a while for Keturah's eyes to adjust to the room. She ducked to go under a low part of the ceiling and then stood next to her father.

He lifted his head and looked toward the door. "What's happened?"

Caleb went to into the darkened room and paced back and forth. "I'll be going to Mizpah to represent our tribe, just southwest of Bethel. Shiloh needs representatives."

"For what?"

Caleb eyed Keturah warily and then looked back at his father. "For something she shouldn't hear."

Keturah let out a sound, scuffing the sweet-smelling reeds scattered about the floor with her sandaled feet. "But, I should know too, especially if it concerns you, Caleb. If I'm woman enough to be watched like a heavily guarded vineyard, then I'm old enough to hear what you have to say."

Her father nodded and looked back at Caleb. "Whatever it is, you can tell it in front of her. We can't protect Keturah from the world forever."

Caleb sighed.

Keturah tapped her sandaled foot against the solid rock floor, making a light sound. "See." But then she stopped, when she realized they were both looking at her.

Caleb stared at her, annoyed, and made a sound. He turned his back to Keturah. "They're meeting at Mizpah to find out why a man from one of the tribes sent them something, and what the meaning of it was. They don't understand how he could do a thing so gruesome. He'll be there to explain it."

Keturah's father clasped his hands in front of him. "What did he send?"

Caleb lowered his voice to almost a whisper. "A terrible thing, pieces of his concubine. She was severed to bits. One part to each of the twelve tribes."

Keturah placed her hand on the wall of stone next to her. "Oh." She wasn't expecting this. A queasy feeling struck her deep inside. Her brother was right. It was not news she could bear easily.

Caleb went to her and took her hand. "I tried to warn you."

Their father looked at Keturah. His brows furrowed. And then he turned back to his son. "Did you find out why he sent this?"

Caleb shook his head. "No. But, I know they'll tell us at Mizpah."

"So, you're going for sure?

"Yes, with Asher. And a group of the Ephraimites from Shiloh."

"Asher?" Keturah put her hand on Caleb's arm, tugging at the sleeve of his robe. "But Caleb, he's only twelve."

Caleb looked at her askew. "Keturah. I was much younger than he was, when I went with father to a meeting there."

Her father nodded. "He's almost a man, and I don't want Caleb going there without family." He shrugged. "Besides. Asher needs to see things outside of Shiloh. There must be representatives from Ephraim. Caleb's nineteen and will care for him."

Keturah groaned. "But Asher was going to help me with the sheep's wool." She knew it was a poor excuse, but worth a try.

"I'll do it. You don't need him."

"But..."

Her father's voice was resolute. "Keturah, you've said enough."

Keturah sighed. She bent her head, knowing better than talking back to her father.

"Now, finish the wool, so Caleb and I can talk."

"Yes, father." She nodded her head obediently. She pushed her dark braid over her shoulder and turned to go back down the stairs. She wanted to stay and argue, but knew it would do no good. Caleb would be leaving with Asher, and there was nothing she could do about it.

***

Joash pushed the stone hoe into the ground making straight rows for planting wheat. The last week of work had been going well. He looked up when he spotted his father on his way out to the field.

"Your mother wants to see you."

Joash stood up. He stopped working, to watch his father approach. "Why? What does she want, now?"

His father used a walking stick to steady himself, as he made his way out to the field. He hesitated at first, but then spoke quietly. "There's another woman with her, she wants you to meet. Naomi."

Joash wiped the sweat from the front of his tunic and dragged the hoe further down the path. He shook his head and then let out a light laugh. "Tell mother I've work to do. We need to get this done. She knows it."

"Joash. You should at least try, for your mother's sake. She does this for you."

"I don't need her help, father. Please." Joash shook the hair from his eyes. He let out a breath.

Simeon pushed his stick firmly in the ground, holding himself there. "It's past time you to take a wife. It is important to preserve our name through children. You should listen."

Joash rolled his eyes. "I've heard all this before." He looked out over the fields and wiped his brow. "But, like I said, I've no time for it. And *if* I take a wife, it'll be for what I want, and in my time, and mother will stay out of it."

Joash's father sighed. "You should pray to the Lord. He'll send you the right one, in the right time. I'll pray and hope you'll see the Lord's goodness."

Joash shook his head. A half smile formed on his face. "You can pray. But, I've no time for that, either."

His father looked at the ground. "None of the young men are listening to the Lord. They go their own way and do what they feel is right, you among them."

"Father...please. I said I don't want to hear it. I told you I've no time for these things." He turned back to his work.

Joash's fist tightened. Why must his father always bring this subject up? And what would a wife bring but more strife? He wanted none of it, not about to trust a woman again.

"Your mother will be disappointed. But, I'll look for an excuse. I see that nothing I say matters, and you aren't willing to listen." He turned and walked away, using the stick in his hand as a guide.

Joash let out a breath, eying his father move slowly across the field. If his mother would only leave things to him and let him worry about it, he might find a way to satisfy them. And yet, it tired him to think of it.

*****

"Then all the children of Israel went out, and the congregation was gathered together as one man, from Dan even to Beersheba, with the land of Gilead, unto the Lord in Mizpah." Judges 20:1 King James's Version

Chapter 4

Keturah's brother dusted off his striped robe and the fur he'd slung over his shoulder. He wiped the grit and grime from his tunic. He and Asher had traveled far on the paths from Shiloh, and he couldn't wait to get to a place where they could finally bathe. Caleb was standing near his brother in a large crowd of men. The meeting place overlooked the rocky platform at Mitzpah, a position where enemies could be spotted miles away in valley below. Trekking across the lush, green mountains rising up on all sides were a daunting task itself.

Luckily in this crowd, he and Asher were able to get a place close enough to the front. Even so, he still had to strain to hear over the sounds of shuffling sandaled feet and the confusion of thousands of armored men behind him.

Caleb eyed the man at the front of the crowd who was from the tribe of Levi. His hair was a mess. His eyes were like hot coals, and his cloak was torn. He lifted his arms, and his robe caught the breeze, flapping in the wind.

"Brothers!" His voice cracked as he called out.

He choked on his words, hanging his head. "Israel needs to know why I sent what I did to your tribes. For my concubine's sake...and for yours."

Caleb felt something wrench inside him at the pained expression in the other man's eyes. There must have been good reason for someone who cared for the tabernacle, to do what he had, a Levite, none-the-less?

The man lowered his arms, and tore his tunic again, smearing ashes on his tear-stained face. The wailing sound he made was mournful and low.

He began choking on his next words, tears still forming trails down his reddened face. "You must all know what those murderers in Gibeah did. When I sent those hideous parcels, it was so everyone in Israel would know the horror I felt, when I saw my concubine the next morning, and learned of the things that went on that night. No one should get away with such indecency. I loved her very much."

The crowd was silent, every eye on him. Their mouths were grim. A few of them, laid their hands on their swords to quiet the clanking sounds at their sides.

Caleb shook his head, puzzled. The man looked spent and as if he'd been crying for days, clearly distraught. How could anyone have brought this man so low? What were they thinking?

Overhead, clouds were gathering, even though the air around them was stagnant. It looked as if later there might be a storm. Sun shadows fell over the distant hills.

The man's voice lowered to a whisper. "I stayed for the night as a guest in an old man's home in the city of Gibeah, in which we talked, nothing untoward. It was actually what I would call an enjoyable evening."

He put his hand to his head, as if pained. "But, then that same night, a gang of men came in the dark and they were loud, beating on the door. The old said they pleaded for him to hand me over to them, so that they could abuse me. But he wouldn't do it. So, instead, to satisfy their lust and send them on their way without any more trouble, I was forced to hand them my concubine, as I knew no other course to take. Other than, the old man giving them his virgin daughter."

He dropped to the floor, weeping, overcome with grief, his deep blue robe forming a puddle around him. "I loved her so."

The crowd of men shifted uneasily, as they watched him. Caleb wondered at how much he loved her, allowing her to take his place.

A man, closest to the Levite went over and put his hand on the man's shoulder. His voice was hard. "What do you want done. We can help. We see you're grieved, in the most disturbing way."

The Levite's eyes fixed on the hills in the distance. "I should feel joy here at Mitzpah, the Holy City. But today, I only feel bitterness and rage. Nothing so terrible has ever been done in Israel."

The Levite took a breath and wiped sweat from his forehead. "She was dead the next morning, lying on the doorstep, her hand stretched over the threshold. She'd been brutalized to the highest degree, and words can't describe the atrocities done to her. She was left beaten, bruised, torn and lifeless. This band of wicked men mistreated her over the course of the night and left her out there to die."

He wiped tears drying on his face. "And I think they should also die for this, for what they did, or it won't be the end of it. There should be consequences, or there'll be more to come. The city's wicked. They turned against their own people."

A man in the back shook his head. "It'll be our wives next! If this deed is left unpunished, no place will be safe!"

A murmur echoed through the crowd and another man shouted. "Someone should be taken to task over it!" All of them chanted in one unified sound.

Then, the Levite lifted his arm and put out his hand. "Hear me out. As I said before, I believe there'll be no end to it, if you refuse to do anything."

The man next to him turned and looked at the crowd. "He's right, you know. It won't end here, if we let them get away with it. We really shouldn't travel back to the safety of our homes, until there's justice for this. We should go to Gibeah and ask the Benjamites to hand these men over, as it happened in their territory."

They all chanted in unison, angrily holding up their spears, and nodding in agreement.

Caleb felt the trepidation inside him, but cast the feeling aside.

Asher looked at his brother. "We'll surely need to go, for the sake of our families, regardless of this man's shameful part in it."

Caleb nodded. "I'll send word home, it may be some time before we're able to make the journey back."

*****

"So all the men of Israel were gathered against the city, knit together as one man." Judges 20:11 King James's Version

Chapter 5

Keturah's stomach felt as if it were in knots when she found out her brothers were headed to Gibeah. What if they ended up in the fight? What was Caleb thinking to bring Asher there?

A lump formed in her throat, and she felt sick. She couldn't think of it.

"It'll be over soon, Keturah." Tirzah patted her on the arm. "They never fight long."

Keturah looked defeated. She took small steps over the hard, rocky path to the tent of meeting behind the rest of her family.

It was quiet this Sabbath day. The mud-brick homes they passed were empty, and people weren't in their courtyards. Instead, they were out on the path with their families, making their way to the synagogue in solemn thought or talking quietly.

The occasional sputter or bellowing wail of a camel rang out over the valley below and sheep bleated quiet, low sounds from the pastures. Aside from that, there was little movement.

Keturah was having a difficult time keeping her mind on the Lord this day. "They left Mitzpah a couple days ago. I only hope the Israelites will be able to get this whole thing settled without difficulties."

Tirzah took her arm, guiding her along. "I am sure of it." Her look was comforting. "As long as the Benjamites hand over those terrible men who killed that poor woman, everything will work out in the end."

Keturah nodded. "I have to believe they will. So, maybe things will be solved peacefully, and my brothers will both be back again, soon."

Tirzah smiled. "It's sure to happen. So don't worry, Keturah."

Keturah looked ahead. The tent of meeting was just down the road.

She didn't speak, as they neared the entrance to the tabernacle where the Lord's presence was. She caught the heavy scent of incense, as she stood outside the tent. The white curtains of fine linen hung from pillars lining the rectangular structure, were taut and sturdy, fastened with ropes. The wall loomed taller, as she approached.

She covered her head, a secure feeling enveloping her and filling her with a sense of peace. Shiloh was blessed to have the Lord's tent with them in her city. Today, she'd pray for protection for her brothers.

*****

"Why do the heathen rage, and the people imagine a vain thing? The kings of the earth set themselves, and the rulers take counsel together, against the Lord, and against his anointed…" Psalm 2:1-2 King James Version

Chapter 6

Joash frowned. "What did they think they were doing, going to war over a concubine? The whole thing's ludicrous," he muttered to himself. And why hadn't his people just turned the men over to them? Couldn't they figure out who did this gruesome thing?

He let out a grunt. As far as he was concerned, the only women he'd bother to fight for were his mother and sister, and they were safe with him in Bethel. Others weren't worth the trouble.

And from what he'd heard, these so-called godly men, didn't even pray over their decision to come out to Gibeah with such demands. And they met at Mitzpah, no less? Wasn't it supposed to be a place of prayer? Ha!

And yet, in these days, it was hit and miss when it came to actual devotion and consultation to the Lord. Even he knew that. Every man did as he saw fit. His father was the only one he knew who truly believed in any of it. The rest, including him, only paid it lip service.

He picked up his woven shield and clothed himself fully in his leather armor. His sling lay on the table where his mother sat.

She stared at him through teary eyes.

"Every Benjamite soldier has to be there, mother." He went over to her and put his hand on her shoulder. He squeezed her gently. "Remember, I'm one of the prized-left handers, as they keep saying. As long as I have my sling, I'll come back to you." He gave her a reassuring grin.

His mother sprung from the table and threw her arms around his shoulders. "Oh, Joash. I know you're strong, and I'll see you again." She began to weep, holding him tightly for a time. "I know you'll return."

Then she leaned back and readjusted his woven, leather breastplate over his chest. She laid her hand on his arm, sighing. "Why couldn't you have been fine-boned and weak, a sickly child?" Her eyes glistened. She looked out over the field, eying the neighbor's son, a thin, young man, plowing the ground with a stone hoe.

He laughed. "Ha! You would have wished that upon me?" His grin was lop-sided, revealing rows of straight, white teeth. "I would've died, first."

She hugged him closer. "Joash. I'd no idea that being a mother would feel like this when you were a little boy. You're strong, blessed in so many ways. I pray every day the Lord will care for you and keep you safe. I'll always do this for you."

He laughed again. "The Lord. Oh, mother. I'll come back soon. You'll see." He didn't look at her, reticent to see the misery in her eyes.

When he could wait no longer, he pulled himself from her and stroked her hair. "Don't worry. It won't be long. Now, I need to tell father to take you and Nissa somewhere safe in Ephraim, until this is all over. It's time. I'll find my way home again soon."

She stood back, watching him with solemn eyes, her hand on her chest.

He knew it wasn't only that he was leaving that made her sad. She had that look again, the one that said she wanted him to love the Lord like she did. But he just didn't see any sense in it. He took his sling off the wooden table next to him, grabbed his spear and sword, and gave her one last fleeting look, heading out the door.

Well, if it gave her hope, she could have her prayers. He supposed it was doing some good. But, for him, he had no time for such things.

***

Nissa eyed her brother from a corner of the courtyard. She watched him leave, but hid so she wouldn't have to face him. He probably would have chided her for not speaking to him, like he almost always did. But, he should know that she still wasn't brave enough to say anything aloud to him. She wasn't ready for such a thing.

She wished she had the courage like he wanted her to, but somehow the words wouldn't come. From the time she was a small child, she found them caught in her throat, and not able to find their way out.

She watched her brother mount his huge, black mare. He got up so easily onto its back, as if he were made for it. No one could deny that he looked every part the soldier he was. His well-defined shoulders and arms from all the training he did, and the way he sat upright with such confidence on his horse, dared anyone to think less.

Most times, she felt afraid of him, the way he taunted her and bellowed loudly to try and get her to talk. He seemed to think this would be the best way to deal with her situation, but he was the one member of the family she felt the least confident around. Deep down, she knew he did it for her own good, and that he really did care for her, as she knew he had a gentle side he tried to hide. But the way he went about it, just seemed to make it worse.

She smiled as she watched him pat the side of his horse and speak gently to it. He was so good with the animals. He had a soft spot for them.

He turned and saw her watching him.

Nissa's cheeks grew rosy as she waved.

His brow rose slightly, and he shook his head. "Be good to mother."

She nodded, staring solemnly at him.

Then he took the reins in his hand and tapped the animal's side, making his way out into the valley. Soon after, his horse was racing across the fields into the distance, and she could no longer see him. As difficult as he could be, she knew she'd miss her brother until he was back again. She always felt safer when he was around.

She sighed, turning to go inside. Mother would surely need her now, so she'd pray for both her and Joash, and for his return.

*****

"And they found among the inhabitants of Jabesh-gilead four hundred young virgins…and they brought them unto the camp to Shiloh…"
Judges 21:12 King James's Version

Chapter 7

Keturah and Tirzah stood at the side of the road.

Keturah's mouth opened. A procession was entering the city! There must have been a hundred or more soldiers bringing carts filled with young Mannassite women from the city of Jabeth Gilead to Shiloh.

Donkeys quietly plodded along, the wheels of their wagons rattling as they passed. Keturah couldn't believe how many women there were. The baskets that hung from the sides of the carts swung freely in the wind, a telltale sign that much of their food had been eaten and most of them very likely had empty stomachs.

"Look, Tirzah." A breath escaped her, and she held her hand to her throat. "They're grieving for their loved ones. They've lost everything."

She stared at the ashes smeared on the women's faces and on the front of their tunics. Most of them were on their knees weeping. One woman looked as if she hadn't slept for days. Others were staring numbly at the fields, clutching tightly to each other and holding their scarves on their heads. At least four hundred of them were being escorted to Shiloh, as their whole city had been destroyed.

Tirzah looked shocked. "What have our Israelite men done? Would the Lord have condoned such a thing? Look at those poor girls? What are they going to do with them?"

"I don't know."

It tore at Keturah's heart to see the expressions on the young women's faces. They looked close to her age, their parents and family killed. They'd been loaded onto the carts like cattle and brought to Shiloh to face an uncertain future. She couldn't imagine anything like that happening to her.

Tirzah looked to wear the women were. "Some of the Mannessite men from their city should've gone to that first meeting at Mizpah. Every city was supposed to send someone to represent them."

Keturah nodded. "Yes, Caleb and Asher told me they didn't show up and that there'd be trouble because of it. And now, Jabesh-Gilead's burned to the ground, and their family's are all gone."

"They're devastated." Tirzah put her hand to her chest.

Keturah looked further down the street. Caleb was there, handing coins to a man for a small, white goat. At least he and Asher were home safe and hadn't been injured in the other city in the Benjamite territory. She'd been so afraid for them. She couldn't count how many prayers she said and how much fasting she did, and was glad the Lord had answered by bringing them back to her.

Had these young women remembered to pray? Their lives had taken a bad turn, and it didn't seem that the Lord was pleased with them.

Tirzah sighed. "I can't begin to understand how they must feel. But, at least the Mannessite tribe only lost one city, and these women were spared. From what I'm hearing, the Benjamite tribe was not so lucky. They were almost all destroyed."

Keturah nodded. "Other than the men who fled, the group of prize-left handers we always heard so much about. Their families are all gone, give or take a few who might have been out of the territory, which I'm sure were hardly any."

She looked at the field in the distance. Tents were set up and the procession of wagons was stopping there. The young women got out of the carts and either went into tents or sat on mats in front of them, pulling swatches of fabric over their heads or wrapping them tightly around their shoulders, rocking back and forth. Even from this far away, their muffled sobs and mournful cries carried over the field.

Tirzah took the clay water jar she filled at the well and lifted it to her shoulder. She looked away from the place where the women were.

She sighed. "Did Caleb tell you anything about what happened to the Benjamite warriors?"

"The left-handers?"

Tirzah nodded.

Keturah eyed her older brother on the path ahead of them. He was carrying the young goat he'd purchased and talking to Asher. The animal's front legs were over his shoulders. "He said the left-handers were forced into the desert at the Rock Rimmon, about six hundred of them. They're hiding there now. It's not many, though. Hundreds of thousands of their men died, along with their families."

"Imagine." Tirzah bit her lip. "One of the twelve tribes, almost wiped out. I wonder how long they'll be able to sustain themselves?'

Keturah shook her head. "Probably not long where they're at, with hardly a woman from their tribe left." She sighed. "How awful it must be in the desert, knowing they've lost their loved ones and may themselves die soon. Eleven tribes, just doesn't seem like something the Lord would have wanted for us."

The last of the carts full of the young women, passed in the direction of a camp in the middle of a large field.

Keturah tugged at Tirzah to move off the path. "There's another wagon, not with them."

Tirzah jumped to the side. "The road's busy."

The driver snapped a whip at his donkey as he passed, and the animal let out a loud bray, quickening his step. The man smiled a toothless grin at them as he drove by. His dusty striped robe, led Keturah to believe he'd been on the trail a while, likely him and those with him, were travelers from another town.

Keturah waved, watching the cart roll past.

Two women inside the back of it lifted their hands and waved back. The wagon gave a lurch and rocked forward. The women grabbed the sides of it smiling.

Keturah's mother made her way to both young women, as they turned to leave. "We'll bring supplies for them." She looked out over the field. "It's the least we can do."

Keturah shook her head. "I'd like that, mother."

Her mother smiled. "I'll stay longer and try to be of help to them." She looked down the road. "But, you need to go back to the house with Tirzah now."

"Yes. I'll wait for you there."

Her mother shook her head and began walking back to the camp.

Keturah turned, as they started for home. "I hope my mother will allow me to give them one of my tunics. It's older, but fresh and clean. Those poor women looked as if they only had the clothes on their backs."

Tirzah smoothed out the folds of her skirt. "Oh. I'll ask if I might do the same."

Keturah smiled. "I'm hoping they're treated well."

"Yes. After all they've been through, they'd better be."

A New Dance

They walked down the narrow path to Keturah's home where Betsalel trotted out from the stone gate to greet them.

Keturah lifted her goat into her arms and ruffled the top of its head. "Hello, little one."

Betsalel struggled out of her hold and quickly jumped back down. He began to eat some grass nearby.

Keturah and Tirzah watched with tender expressions.

Tirzah switched the water jar to her other shoulder. "So I'll meet you, tomorrow?"

"Tomorrow, yes." Keturah's eyes sparkled.

They waved goodbye and headed off in different directions.

*****

"But six hundred men turned and fled to the wilderness unto the rock Rimmon, and abode in the rock Rimmon four months." Judges 20:47 King James's Version

Chapter 8

Joash stood at the crest of a conical and very prominent rocky hill in the middle of the desert. A hot, grueling dust rushed over him, depositing grit into his mouth. Four months of living in this infernal hotbed was about all he could take. He put his hand on his sling and let out a groan.

How had things gotten so out of control?

"How many of us are left?" He turned to his commander and friend, Cyrus.

Cyrus was standing next to Joash, looking about as miserable as he was. "About six hundred."

Joash scowled. "We'll surely all die in this place, and the tribe, too. We've no one to carry on our name. They've killed everyone." His brows knit tightly together. For the first time in his life, he began to think about why his parents felt so adamant about him taking a woman. But now, it might be too late.

Cyrus sighed. "It's impossible to think that the Lord's plan was for the Benjamite clan to die out, cut off from the others."

"Humph! I wouldn't have thought so, either. But, after this time in the desert, I'm beginning to wonder." Joash began to laugh dryly and shake his head. "And it doesn't surprise me that we're in this accursed place over a woman."

He wiped at the sweat trickling down his neck, breathing in another mouthful of hot air, agitated. "No one even knew who hurt that concubine. They said it happened in the middle of the night. What other course could we have taken?"

Cyrus drummed his fingers against his tunic. "Not a whole lot, but stand our ground and fight."

Joash shrugged, clenching his fist and eying the hills in the distance. "We should never have left the city to do it."

Cyrus nodded. "We were winning before then." He looked over the hills. "But, you're right. If we could've held on and stayed put, maybe things wouldn't have went the way they had."

A New Dance

A hollow, sick feeling sunk deep into Joash's stomach. How had everything fallen to such disrepair? Now, they were cut off from not only their land, but also from the other tribes of Israel.

There had been no word from his parents, and he didn't even know if they were still alive. He couldn't imagine what they were going through, and didn't want to think of what happened to them if they weren't. At least he'd advised them to leave the Benjamite territory. It may have saved their lives. "Not much good it does us now, to keep wondering. What's done is done."

Cyrus nodded. "It's true."

Joash went to one of the cave entrances to try and get some shade and a drink of water. At least inside the cave he'd find some solace from the blistering rays. Later, when it cooled down, it would be a good time to go after some food.

He'd had enough of the hot sand and scorpions, and wondered what the men would do now. How would they sustain themselves with no prospects in sight? What would it be like for them if they perished in this dry hotbed, without even a battle wound or a fight?

***

Keturah eyed the camp on the outskirts of the city from the edge of the road. The empty basket slung over her shoulder, weighed her down on one side. At least she'd been able to do her part to contribute. During the past months, the women eagerly accepted the food and provisions she and other village people brought them. They were outwardly thankful.

There was movement today, though. Soldiers were at Shiloh, and they were loading the young Mannessite women from the camp back onto carts. It'd been months since they first arrived, and now they were being taken elsewhere.

They gripped tightly to their baskets and woven blankets they'd made during their stay in Shiloh, along with food and supplies for the trip.

"Where do you plan to take them?" An older woman eyed the soldiers curiously.

One of the men turned. "The Benjamite territory. "Then, we're going to the desert and bringing the warriors out of there."

"The left-handers?" The woman's face lit.

The man nodded. "Yes. We figured we should've prayed when we were at Mizpah and things wouldn't have turned out the way they did. It'll be better this way. Otherwise, the tribe will be lost to us. These women can be their wives, as they've no fathers to give them away."

The woman's expression was solemn. "Oh, I suppose it'll be a good thing for them in the end. There will be heirs this way, and the Benjamites will treat them well."

Keturah didn't say anything, but stared across the field, eying the stony expressions on the young women's faces.

It was a surely a good thing these women had a place to go with the Benjamite men to care for them? At least they'd be with other Israelites and would have homes again.

Something gnawed at her insides, though. She wondered how she'd feel, if she'd watched her parents die in front of her and then was taken from her home, and handed over to men from a tribe she didn't know.

Her expression was grave, as she eyed the carts roll out of town. What would it have been like to experience the horrific things these women had and then face an unknown future?

She couldn't imagine being taken from Shiloh, across stretches of wild country, to become the wife of a man, not of her parent's choosing. None of them would have any idea what kind of man they'd get.

She couldn't wait for her engagement to Hiram to take place, because after that she'd not have to worry about such things. The Lord would care for her and would do what was best.

*****

"And the whole congregation sent some to speak to the children of Benjamin that were in the Rock Rimmon, and to call peaceably unto them." Judges 21: 13 King James's Version

Chapter 9

Joash squinted and raised his hand to his forehead. Aside from the consummate dust and hot wind, something else seemed to be making its way over the horizon. The bright orange desert sun couldn't hide the thunderous sound of camel's feet.

Were the other Israelite tribes coming to finish them off? His grip tightened on his sling. At least he'd fight, if it came to that.

The sound grew louder. His heart beat steady in his chest, and his eyes narrowed trying to weigh the intentions of the men headed their way. He adjusted his breastplate.

The steamy haze brought the camels closer, and the sounds grew louder. Joash held his breath at the camels advancing headlong at a rapid pace. Eleven brightly colored banners flew high above them, and the sounds of trumpets began to blow.

He was right. It was the other tribes. The vibrations of the earth reverberated loudly beneath them, until all the racing camels, finally stopped within about fifty horse lengths.

The pounding and thunderous noise suddenly quieted, as the riders lined the hills with rows of camels. There was silence, broken only by an animal's occasional mournful bellow. Hot dust made from their large monstrous hooves clouded the hazy sky behind them.

Some of the men waiting for word, in the rising vapors of the sun, took their water flasks and raised them to their lips, taking slow deliberate sips. Three of them in the front, lifted their arms, and waved cloth banners.

And then Joash heard it, the call of peace, faint at first, but then louder like the sound of a trumpet, ringing throughout the valley.

No one responded, but all of them stared, dry-mouthed at their Israelite brothers.

Suddenly, one of the Benjamites yelled. "A truce is what they're asking for!"

Joash let out a breath and loosened his fist on his weapons. None of the soldiers from his tribe would've been in any kind of shape to fight, after living the way they had for months.

The men got off their camels, drawing them nearer and stepping into the camp. Joash unfastened his breastplate, pulling it from his head. Then, he lay it on the hot sand and put down his spear and sling.

His fellow soldiers were worn down, beaten by the fiery temperatures, and ready to welcome any favorable gesture from the other Israelite tribes, any sign that they might leave this place.

Joash scanned the hills in the distance, and something in him stirred. If his parents took his advice and went outside of the Benjamin territories to stay until all this came to pass, maybe they were still alive. He'd be checking the border towns, as soon as he got the chance. He groaned at the thought of others who remained in the territory, all wiped out.

"It's over." A man from one of the other tribes called out, his voice choking. "We want no more retribution to come against you, as we believe the Lord's plan did not include, wiping out one tribe."

The rest of them began to weep. "We're brothers again."

The prize left-handers threw their arms around their fellow Israelites, clapping them on their backs and shaking hands.

Joash couldn't wait to get out of the hot sands and back to his homeland. He sighed with relief; glad for the celebrating that had begun to take place. Everyone relaxed for the first time since they'd ended up in the desert, and there were tears of joy staining more than one man's cheeks. The anticipation of going home was etched in each soldier's face.

After the excitement died down, there was a lull in the conversation.

"This is all good news, I don't doubt it," one man quietly stated. Then, a frown drew over his brow, and he looked around him. "But, has anyone considered what we're going to do, after we get back to our homeland?"

No one answered.

The man's voice was louder, more insistent. "How do we sustain our tribe without our women? We heard about the vow taken to the Lord, that no Israelite would give us he daughter. How can our tribe carry on this way? It'll surely be the end of us."

Another man from a different tribe in the back stepped forward. "This time, we prayed to the Lord, and found a way to help you."

He smiled. "You're surely our brothers, and the design of the Lord was for us to have twelve tribes. In our sin, we realized we'd done so much wrong, and we're prepared to make amends."

The Benjamites looked skeptical.

Someone else called out, "But the Lord wouldn't be pleased, if this vow to him were broken."

The man agreed. "It's true. We can't break the solemn vow." He hesitated. "But, there were four hundred young women, taken from the city of Jabeth Gilead."

Then he shook his head. "So much has happened." He eyed the men there with a saddened expression. "When the Manassite men didn't show up at the meeting at Mizpah, their people were cut down because of their disobedience, other than these young women who were not. Now, we believe the Lord preserved them for this purpose, even though we erred in our ways."

He held his hands out in an open gesture. "The women have no homes. They've no place to go to, no parents to secure their future. So, in taking them, your tribe won't die out, and they'll have husbands to protect them. If we do this, we won't have broken our vow. All their people are dead, and there are none to speak for them."

One Benjamite wiped a tear from his face. "So many deaths, and to what purpose?" He let out a breath and nodded. "We've no other choice and will care for these women as our own. The Lord has done great things, despite our sins."

There was a collective sigh, and a huge cheer reverberated throughout the camp.

The tension in Joash's shoulders relaxed, and his closed fist released at the man's news. Their tribe would survive.

The sun lowered in the sky, as it neared the horizon. Night was coming. It'd be good to camp during the late sun hours and then set out for home in the dark before the heat took over again. One more day in the cave was all he'd have to endure. He couldn't wait to be going.

*****

"Then he said unto him, Come home with me, and eat bread." I Kings 13:15 King James's Version

Chapter 10

Joash rode into the next town between rows of small brick homes. He stopped to watch a shepherd boy, driving sheep across the path. His body tensed as he waited for the wooly animals to clomp slowly past.

The anticipation to see his family was so great he could barely wait for the last sheep to cross. The horse snorted and pawed at the dirt and seemed to sense his wish to get moving. He held the reigns firmly.

The noonday sun beat down on him, and he took time to tie a long cloth over his head with a leather cord to shade the back of his neck. He scanned the horizon for more homes.

The area he searched was hilly, and the towns were small.

He'd spent months looking for his mother, father and Nissa and went to every place near the border he could think of, but hadn't heard anything of their whereabouts. He was nearing his friend's home and was sure this was where his family would be.

When the last of the sheep trooped across the road, Joash tapped his heels into the side of his horse and then made a clucking noise. The great animal moved forward down the path, kicking up dust behind them.

Further down the road, Joash got off his horse and began to walk, guiding the animal further. His eyes lit on the branches of a large Acacia tree that spread out over the path. Another house was just around the bend.

Maybe he'd find them? Spared from the war.

As he rode further down the path, he spotted a cave-like home, built into a rocky wall jutting out from the side of a hill. It was partially hidden from view, his friend's home. A woman was in the outer courtyard working on a loom.

Joash quickly tied his horse to a tree, taking great strides the rest of the distance and into the courtyard.

His mother lifted her head as he approached, and a sparkle lit her eyes. She reached for him and let out a sound.

He took her in his arms in a crushing embrace. "I thought I might never see you again." He breathed a sigh of relief, knowing she was still alive and that his father and sister would be, too.

She ruffled his dark hair, and tears fell freely down her face. "With only six hundred men left, I was losing hope. But I knew you were a survivor."

Joash hugged his father and sister after they came out of the home.

"Son." His father took his arm. There were tears in his eyes. "We were beginning to have our doubts."

Nissa sighed, relief visible in her eyes. She took her brother's arm and laid her head against it.

Joash shook his head when he looked at her. And then he took her hand. He reached up with the other hand and smoothed back her hair. "There's a place I've secured, for us to go to." He put his arm to his side. "There were so many empty homes and so few of us left, we were able to take what we wanted. We'll be living well."

Joash's father sighed. "It's one blessing, with so much sadness."

"Yes." Joash agreed. "It's a large estate with hundreds of sheep and goats, in Bethel. There's a lot of room for us now, and we can live there very comfortably. Tomorrow, we'll pack and set out for it."

His father took his arm. "You don't know how happy we are that you've returned. We were praying."

Joash eyes glittered sardonically. "To the Lord, who allowed this tragedy to happen?" He lifted his chin.

"No, Joash. To the one who saw us through it." His father patted his arm. "Let us get to our rooms. We've quite a journey ahead of us."

Joash shrugged. "I'll get you there in no time."

*****

"Therefore they commanded the children of Benjamin, saying Go and lie in wait in the vineyards…" Judges 21: 20 King James's Version

Chapter 11

"It's lovely." Keturah squinted in the bright morning light, waiting for her friend's reply. The warmth of the day felt good, and she reveled in the sun's gentle rays.

Tirzah nodded. She looked up from where she sat on a woven mat in the courtyard of Keturah's home. She was twisting a vine into a circular shape. "We'll lay out the wreaths in a few minutes and let them dry. The other young women can wear them, too."

Keturah lifted a dark braid over her shoulder and took another vine from the pile next to her and began to bend it. She looked up once more from what she was doing and nodded. Her eyes were bright. She fingered the small white flowers she'd woven through the leaves. The petals were soft, and their scent was heavenly. She couldn't wait. The annual festival of the Lord in Shiloh was going to be celebrated in a couple of days.

Finally, she'd be able to dance to the Lord in front of everyone. She could freely share with others what she loved so much. Her stomach churned inside with the excitement of it all, and she ached for the day to come.

Tirzah lifted the wreath she was working on, her eyes full of mischief. "This will be what you will be like at the festival, Keturah." She held it up and peered through it, speaking in a playful tone. "Hiram? A few more days, and I'll be your wife!"

Keturah pulled her friend's hand down. "Tirzah! He'll hear you. He's near the gate." She looked toward the arched opening and then to the ground, her cheeks growing hot. She took a breath.

Tirzah got up. She began to giggle, which turned to laughter, turning in the direction the stone entrance. "Hiram? Where?"

Keturah grabbed her friend's tunic and pulled her back down onto the woven mat. "Tirzah…I said to stop."

Tirzah wiggled to get comfortable and then picked up another piece of vine, watching the quiet, mild man, out of the corner of her eye.

Keturah lifted her eyes slightly, eying him curiously. He wasn't a handsome man, yet had a kind enough face, despite it being somewhat weather worn from years of heat and sun beating down on him while he'd worked in the fields. He'd surely be stable in temperament and would be a good provider.

Tirzah sighed. "It's too bad he hasn't changed. And never seems to." She went back to working on her wreath, her mouth turning down at the corners.

"What do you mean by that?" Keturah's cheeks reddened. She rested the vine on her lap holding it there.

Tirzah shrugged. "Oh, I don't know. I suppose he's predictable, what he does, even the expression on his face."

Keturah scolded. "But, surely, you're not being fair. Hiram's dependable."

"Yes. It's true. You'll never have to second guess anything he does."

"Which can be a good thing."

"It can." Tirzah pulled one of the vines through two others, bending them into shapes. "And yet, might prove tiresome over time."

Keturah looked a bit ruffled. "Well, my parents have chosen him, and they'll do what's best for me."

Tirzah sighed. She patted Keturah's arm and handed her the flower, her face suddenly contrite. "Keturah. I didn't mean to make you feel bad. I'm sure he'll be a fine husband. Your parents would do the best thing for you."

Keturah took a flower and sighed, lifting it to her nose to breathe in its light, sweet scent. "I think so, too. They plan to tell him their answer the night of the festival, and I'm sure it'll be a good match."

Tirzah went back to her work, nodding. "Yes. Don't listen to me, the dreamer."

Keturah smiled. "You know I wouldn't." And then she giggled. "But, even though I know what I should do, I have my own dreams, too."

Tirzah blinked. "You do?"

Keturah laughed. "Everyone does. Most of the time they're good ones. But, then others I need to let go of, as they might get a dutiful Hebrew girl into trouble, like my dancing."

Tirzah smiled and then added with a snort. "You go ahead and keep being that sweet, obedient daughter for your parents. At least you'll live in Shiloh and do well."

Keturah nodded. "Yes. And this is what I want the most."

***

Joash let out a breath, shaking his head. He brushed the dust off the side of his horse, readying himself to mount. Shouldn't this finally have made his father happy? Isn't it what both his parents wanted all along?

"Please, Joash. It surely isn't what the Lord would wish for you."

Joash stared out over the hills in the distance. The sun rose over the house behind him, shining across the valley of light brown rock, deepening the shadows from the slant of its rays. He'd have to get started now, to get there in time. "The Israelites said this would be good for the tribe and that we can sustain our heritage this way. It'll work out in the end."

Joash's father looked disheartened. "But, did they consult the Lord about it?"

Joash frowned. "I wasn't there, so how would I know, father?"

"And you believe it's a good thing?"

"How could it not be?" Joash picked up his sling and adjusted the leather straps around his horse's neck. "I wasn't here when they brought those Mannessite women. But, there were only four hundred of them. There are six hundred of us. What other way is there? To marry a woman who isn't an Israelite, which you wouldn't want? And what good would that be?"

He drummed his fingers against his side. He couldn't understand his father's reluctance. There really wasn't any other way.

His father shook his head. "Too many sins are being committed. We need a king, a godly one, to lead us to the Lord and from doing wrong."

Joash mounted his horse and looked down. "But for now, there is none. So, it's all right to do as we see fit. You'll see, father. It'll all work out."

Simeon shook his head again, looking disheartened. "Why you've never listened to sense, it's difficult for me to understand."

Joash didn't respond at first. Something churned in him.

He sat up straighter on the horse and gave a rueful smile. "I don't think I see things the same as you do, father." And then he grinned. "Mother's been wanting this for me for a long time. She'll finally have her way."

He smoothed back the black mane of the horse, his hand gentle upon the back of the great animal's neck.

His father sighed. "You know it isn't what she meant. And I believe if you wait, the Lord will find a way for you."

Joash couldn't help letting out a resounding laugh. "Ha!" He snorted. "The Lord?" Then he laughed again. "You of all people should know I'm not one to wait patiently for something to happen. There'll be no repercussions with this. You'll see."

He refused to meet his father's eyes, when the older man answered quietly. "Maybe not with the other Israelites, but with the Lord? You should consult him, or there will be consequences. There always is with sin."

Joash rolled his eyes. "I'll be home, soon. And mother will be glad of it. You'll see." He turned the reigns to steer toward the west in the direction of Shiloh and clucked to the horse, not saying anything else. Nothing he could do could change his father's thinking, he was so dead set against what he was doing.

He drove off, bothered to see his father's head bent in prayer.

His mouth formed a grim line. At least his mother and Nissa weren't there trying dissuade him. They wouldn't approve of what he had planned to do either, but would have to get used to the idea. When he returned, things would be different. They'd all eventually have to adjust to the new arrangement.

***

The scent of flowers breathed life into the city of Shiloh. The harvest day finally arrived, and the people gathered their first fruits to bring them to the tabernacle as a sacrifice. Thousands of people all over the city celebrated.

"The Lord's good." Keturah eyes sparkled. "Look at our new tunics and jewelry. They're so beautiful." Her dark hair fell in thick curls down her back, contrasting with the soft yellow in the dress. Her woven belt of white linen showed off the curves about her waist.

"You're beautiful, Keturah." Tirzah reached over and adjusted the wreath on her friend's head. "Hiram will be blessed to have you as his wife. I hope he's what you've wished for."

Keturah nodded. "I know he will be. And I'll live in Shiloh in a good home."

Tirzah reached out and touched the golden jewelry hanging from Keturah's neck. "It's lovely. Did your father give it to you?"

Keturah nodded. "Yes. He wanted me to have it for the festival." She fingered the matching golden armband resting midway between her shoulder and elbow. The festival had been wonderful over the course of the afternoon. It was one of those perfect days for it, with a blue sky spread out over them and soft, white clouds occasionally shadowing them from the sun's tepid rays.

The dancing would begin in the vineyards near their home soon, all over the city in the different gardens. Keturah's heart raced, as Tirzah and her made their way down the hill to the flat place where they'd sway to the sound of the pipes.

Both of the young women grabbed hands and giggled when the music began to play. They swung each other around in circles first and danced in the light of the evening sun.

Then, Keturah let go and turned, lifting her arms to the orange-red sky, letting her dark hair fall freely behind her.

She spun in graceful curves, drinking in the smells of the grapes hanging full on the vines and the scents of flowers spreading ribbons of light perfume in the air. She let herself go, the happiness of the day spilling out from within her. She felt as if she could dance all night.

***

Joash peered through the heavy vineyards, green vines lush with purple grapes. His breath caught in his throat when he spied the young dancer in the center of the field. The beautiful woman, swaying gracefully to the beat of the music in wild abandon, stole his heart.

His father's words stuck with him, but he chose to ignore them. What did the Lord care about this? Wouldn't he want their tribe to flourish and not die out? Men did this all the time in the spoils of war. It would be no different.

And it was the Israelites themselves who were the ones who devised the plan. Only those at Shiloh were left in the dark about the scheme, and for a good cause. The Lord surely couldn't blame them for their ignorance in the matter.

Yet, afterward, when the fathers of the women learned it was the Benjamites who had taken their daughters, they were sure to realize these young women would inherit riches, wealthy estates and large areas of land and would choose not to retaliate. How wrong could it be?

He turned back to the beautiful young woman with the sun-kissed face and soft, dark curls trailing down her back. He needed to act soon, as he wanted her for himself. She'd surely accept her lot once she realized her family would do the same.

He waited until she neared the edge of the garden, and the people from her village around her turned their attentions elsewhere. And then he made his move, along with the other Benjamite men hidden in the bushes.

***

Keturah raised her arms to the Lord, praising his name with her lips against the backdrop of the sweet-smelling vines. The people around her at the festival faded in her mind, as she swirled to the sound of the pipes. What a glorious day it had been.

She was so lost in her thoughts, she didn't notice what was happening around her, until she felt strong arms lifting her into the air and tossing her over a broad shoulder. Although, she kicked and tried to break free, she was carried through a break in the vines and tossed upon a horse.

She began to scream as the man who held her, jumped up behind and clamped his hand around her waist. She struggled wildly, but was unable to budge from his embrace.

Tears sprung to Keturah's eyes. She lowered her head and covered her face with her hands and began to sob. Where was her father? Her brothers? Did they know what was happening? Did they see?

She felt the tight grip around her waist and tried to pry loose the hand that kept her there, but it still wouldn't shift from the spot, as they raced down the hillside and out into the valley below.

The man was taking her from Shiloh. A deep shudder coursed through her, and a sick fear spread deep within her. Her hair whipped across her face, and she pushed it behind her, peering at the horizon. Other horses and camels raced in different directions over the tops of the hillsides adjacent to Shiloh.

Women's cries rang out in the night, and she realized she wasn't the only one taken. She wondered where Tirzah was. She was sure her friend had to have been in the midst of them, too.

The horse was swift, and she couldn't see anyone from the village following, as the darkness closed in around them. Where did these men come from, and who were they? Why hadn't she been watching or at least tried to run? She might have stood a chance.

Her body shook uncontrollably, as the cool night air whipped around her, and they rode further from her family and home. Her heart beat wildly in her chest.

The man suddenly drew her closer, the warmth of his body stealing over her. She tried to push him away, but could do nothing.

Tears ran over her cheeks, and she groaned at the thought of what was to become of her. She remembered the Mannassite women taken as Benjamite wives. Just days before, she'd wondered what it felt like to be handed over in marriage to a strange man, and now things seemed much more real to her as she rode on in the darkness, knowing her fate might not be so different.

*****

"The Lord also will be a refuge for the oppressed, a refuge in times of trouble. And they that know thy name will put their trust in thee: for thou, Lord, hast not forsaken them that seek thee." Psalm 9:9-10 King James Version

Chapter 12

They rode at breakneck speed through the hills of Ephraim over the course of the night. Keturah tried to study the terrain, but the darkness made it near impossible. Other than a sliver of moonlight and the dim stars, all else seemed like shadows and black shapes. She couldn't tell which direction they were going. All she knew was that with each passing hour, she was being taken further and further from Shiloh and all she held dear.

They raced over sands and hills, down rocky paths and past lone trees leaning awkwardly against the night sky. She cringed at the thought of some wild animal or hungry beast overtaking them.

She found no comfort in thinking about what might be in store for her.

How did this happen?

The cool night air covered her arms in chilly bumps, and she shuddered. She'd been praying every day for the Lord to guide her life and care for her. Was this his answer? How could anything like this be the will of the Lord?

As they rode through the night, she began to ache all over. She had a difficult time holding herself upright, but she didn't say anything, as she didn't want to speak to the man who carried her from her family and Shiloh. Her eyelids began to close, and she fought to stay awake. Eventually, she succumbed to her weariness and turned on her side, slipping into a restless sleep.

A couple times in the night, she tried to glance up to see what the man looked like, but could only make out a shadowy side of a face, the cheekbones hard and unrelenting and the jawline set without movement. She noticed a scar running down the length of his cheek. Everything about him seemed dark and grim.

When she finally woke, it was daylight out, and she immediately sat up straight. The terrain had changed. There were less shrubs and greenery and miles of dark, rocky hills stretching for as far as she could see. She noticed there were pouches of water hanging from the sides of the horse. She felt parched, but had to stretch first.

"I need to stop." She tugged on the man's arm.

He slowed the horse near a row of tall shrubs and got down, lifting her onto the ground beside him. Her sandaled feet smashed into the hot sand, and she lost her balance, grasping the horse's side to try and stop from falling.

He took her arm to steady her.

Keturah turned and looked up at him for the first time. Her breath caught in her throat. She guessed he was most likely a soldier by the way he stood, his shoulders at attention and his feet planted slightly apart, hand on his weapon, and by the scar she'd noticed in the night. It appeared, as if his cheek, had been slashed by a sword.

Dark hair fell over his ears in waves, framing a chiseled face, which in better circumstances might have charmed many a women. Yet, Keturah found the fact unsettling and disagreeable. She wanted nothing to do with him. If only she could go back to Shiloh, where she belonged.

She let go and took a step, but after riding for so long was forced to take his arm again to hold herself upright. She let out an aggravated sound.

He watched her curiously, with something akin to amusement in his expression. "It takes time after traveling long."

She looked at him with narrowed eyes. "I'm not a soldier. And have never been on a horse."

He reached out and took a piece of her hair in his hand.

She tried to pull away, but he didn't let go, marveling at the strand. And then he laughed. "No. You certainly look nothing like any of the soldiers."

His grip loosened, and she pulled away.

Her eyes narrowed, and she felt heat rise in her cheeks. She wanted nothing to do with this man and his vileness. "Where can I go for some privacy?"

She wished she could run away, but when she looked around, she realized there was nothing but desolate wilderness surrounding them. She'd surely die if she tried to leave with no food or provisions. But, then maybe it'd be a good thing for her.

He pointed to the shrubs not far from them and remarked casually. "There." And then he put his hand on her arm. "But, it'd be foolish to try to leave. And you wouldn't get far if you did."

Keturah pushed his hand away. She wanted to retaliate, but kept quiet. She headed to the small area scattered with brush. Her sandals were quiet, as she took small steps on the sandy earth to the gnarled bushes.

She eyed the rocky hillside around her. Dust and more dust swirled over what little shrubbery there was. The tepid wind was no comfort, beating down on her with little mercy. A knot formed inside her as she noticed the barrenness of the land that went on for miles. There was nowhere she could run to, no sign of life in this desolate place. No oasis or shelter.

She stood up and stared past the hills out over the horizon. She squinted, watching for anyone who might be nearby who could help, but saw no one. It was as if the rest of civilization had been swallowed up, leaving her alone in this place in the company of a man she wanted nothing to do with.

She shook the dust out of her sandals and hesitated. The man showed no sense of decency. Who could do something like this to another person and then behave as if the whole thing meant nothing to him?

Her hands began to shake, and she tried to hold them still, but couldn't. She clasped them to her, the pulse in her quickening at the thought of what had happened.

She felt the dry heat consuming her body and lifted her scarf higher over her head. She realized she couldn't stay here forever. Her mouth was parched and dry, and she felt weak inside. She turned and reluctantly made her way back, lifting the bottom of her tunic to keep from tripping and watching the path as she walked.

When she returned, the man was leaned up against a lone Acacia tree under its massive shade watching her. He had the same self-satisfied expression as he had before.

She couldn't stop the heat, which came into her face again because of the way he boldly appraised her. She wasn't used to such scrutiny by a man before. She slowed her pace as she neared him, watching him cautiously.

His eyes swept over her, assessing her with relish, and then they rested on her face.

Another flood of warmth rushed to her cheeks, and she turned away, looking across the terrain. She felt slight next to him, because of his extraordinary height and build and the confidence in his expression.

She spoke with as much firmness as she could muster. "I'm ready to leave." Though the shade of the tree felt good compared to the hot sun that beat down on them, she'd no desire to stay alone in this place with him.

A lazy grin spread across his face. "You're not curious as to where we're going?" He handed her a water sack and lifted it to her.

She took a long drink and then pushed it away. She stared at him, noncommittal. She didn't like his pleased expression. Everything about the man unsettled her.

"You don't want to know?" A spark lit his eye.

She brushed the dust off of her tunic and shook out her hair. The heat on her neck from the thickness of it was almost unbearable. "I want to go back. To my home."

He watched her closely, taking the container back from her. "Don't set your hopes on Shiloh, again." He took a drink, letting the water drip down his chin and then swiped it away with his dusty hand. "You'll go with me, now." His dark hair fell forward into his eyes, and he shoved it off of his face. The leather band around his head covering was worn and frayed. He pushed the hair through it.

Keturah stared at him with a look of consternation. He appeared as if he'd been living in the wild his whole life, and she suspected she wasn't far from the truth. She let out a shaky breath. If there were another place she could find shade she would, but the wide, heavily canopied tree was their only comfort for miles, so she was forced to stay under its wide branches next to him.

She thought about what she could say to get him to take her back to Shiloh. He didn't look like a man easily swayed, but it was worth a try.

She suddenly went to him and took his arm. "Please. If you take me back to my parents, they won't take measures against you. They'll honor such a thing."

A humorous gleam lit his eyes, and he eyed her with the same look he had earlier. He lifted her hand and gently turned it in his. "I'm not afraid of what your family will do." His eyes nonchalantly swept the hills around them, as he stood there next to her.

She searched the barren terrain again for miles beyond the other side of the tree, once again, seeing nothing but dust and rock, no end in sight, and her heart wrenched inside her. Anything moving might give her a thread of hope, but the ripple of heat waves was all that stirred on the horizon.

A tear began to drop on her cheek, but she wiped it away. The raw emptiness inside her, made her stomach queasy. "My family will be looking for me. They'll want to know I'm safe."

"They'll know soon enough." He shrugged, not persuaded by her tears. "And might, already. I'm sure once they've digested the information, they'll not be opposed." He watched for her reaction, his lip lifting at the corners.

Her father? Or brothers? Not opposed? How could he say such a thing? Keturah wanted to reach up and wipe the smug expression from his face. He knew nothing of her family. She churned inside with the thought. "You can be sure they won't stand for anything your people have done. Especially, the way it was carried out. You should be looking for my brothers and father, because they aren't going to like it."

He smiled chuckling to himself, infuriating her more. "I suppose I must be ready for them then." He looked nonplussed. "But, as I said before, they'll surely come to see things our way in the end. It might take your father time to get used to the idea, but I believe he'll come around, if he wants what's best for his daughter."

"Best?" Keturah lashed out at him, pushing him on the chest, not caring what he did to her. "How do you know what's best for me?" She felt heat rise again in her cheeks, at the anger suddenly spewing from her, something she was unaccustomed to.

He grinned, a light in his eyes, as if she were only entertainment and what she said had no effect on him.

Keturah clasped her hands in front of her, willing herself not to speak anymore. She wanted to pummel the man with her fists or worse than that. It seemed he had no heart, or one that could not be easily persuaded. There seemed to be nothing she could do to change his mind.

He looked at her, his eyes sparkling. "You want to say something else. So, why do you hold back?"

Her hands lowered in frustration. He was nothing like her family. "I care nothing about who you are, or where we're going." She looked at him with narrowed eyes. "I don't plan to stay with you. I detest everything you stand for and what you did."

He appeared indifferent to her remark, but something told Keturah she'd grazed a nerve.

His voice lowered. "You'll stay, but only because it'd be foolish to do otherwise. Whether you want it or not, you're going to Bethel. We'll be joining the others, in due time."

She turned from him, but he swung her back around. He lifted her chin so that she'd look at him, but she refused to meet his eyes.

His mouth was grim, and she could see the tight edge of his jawline. "It may be of no consequence to you, but I've many possessions and a good home. You'll be well cared for."

Keturah's cheeks turned hot like the desert. "By you? I don't think you'd know the first thing about it."

He patted his horse. "He gets good care." He grinned, his eyes lighting.

Keturah stared blankly at him. A horse? And this is what he was comparing her to? Her stare was icy, and she lifted her chin, not responding.

He laughed, eying her curiously. "What you think is of no consequence to me."

He added. "And my given name is Joash. You can call me this when you're with me."

She grasped his arm in a pleading gesture. "Please. I don't want to know your name, or you. I only want to be back with my family."

Joash chuckled, gently taking her hand. "But, they'll be expecting you to know it, in Bethel." He drew her closer, speaking under his breath. "How would it be, if you didn't even know your own husband's name?"

At first, Keturah's heart felt like it stopped, and she yanked her hand away, pushing him from her. She began to tremble as a weak feeling tore through her, making her sick inside. There was no arrangement made. Or asking her what she wanted. Her parents didn't even know him.

Her mind raced in desperation. She grasped at anything she could think of to say to wipe the self-assured expression off his face. She looked away and half choked on her next words. "But, this isn't possible. The matter's already settled."

His eyes narrowed. "What matter? What are you talking about?"

A fire burned inside Keturah. She turned back defiantly. "It's already arranged. I'm to marry someone else. Hiram, from my village."

Joash blinked. "You're engaged?" For the first time since she met him, he looked slightly shaken. "How long?"

"It will be set, as my father was going to talk to him at the dance. It was decided, though not official, yet."

Joash's brow loosened, and he looked relieved but somewhat annoyed with her for trying to deceive him. He touched her cheek, his eyes never wavering. "You'll forget whatever was to be arranged. We've been together for a night. And even *you* can't deny that. That man's nothing to you and never was. You need to remember that when the dance ended for you, that part of your life ended as well."

Keturah backed away from him. He seemed so sure of his decision without regard to her feelings. It seemed impossible to imagine marrying the type of man who'd treat her as he did.

She pushed her sandal in the steaming sand beneath her and looked down at the ground. "How could anyone do something as this?" She spit the words out, angrily. She practically choked on her words, when she met his dark eyes again. "How?"

He seemed annoyed at having to explain anything to her, but shrugged and spoke in a low tone. "You heard the story…about what happened to us? I'm from the tribe of Benjamin. When the war was over, there were no women and no prospects for us. We had no other choice but to go to Shiloh."

Keturah bristled. "No choice? It's a lie. I heard how your women perished. But also knew you *did* have women to take as wives. The women from Jabeth Gilead were sent to your tribe. Why didn't you take one of them? They had no homes or families. You could've done this, rather than something as deplorable as taking what wasn't yours."

Something flickered in his eyes. "There were four hundred of them and six hundred of us. I wasn't there, when they brought them."

"But, there were enough…"

He shook his head. "No. If there were, I wouldn't have had a need for you."

Her voice shook, and she felt a wave of sickness wash over her, when she realized the futility of her situation.

Joash grunted and looked as if bothered by the whole turn of the conversation. "What does it matter, one way or the other? Your parents would've made arrangements with a man you hardly knew, anyway."

"But, *he* was a good man." Keturah glowered. "Willing to wait for my parent's approval."

Joash observed dryly. "And I'm sure your parents approved of his assets, like the parents with daughters eying me each night at my dinner table. I've no time for that."

"My parents aren't like that." Keturah's face flamed.

"All of them look over a man's possessions for their daughter and for themselves. This is how they make their choice. There was little difference in what I did, eying a women at the dance, looking for the qualities I desired." His grin widened.

She bristled at his remark. "But, you don't know me. And you're wrong about my parents. They knew Hiram. You sound as if you were acquiring a horse."

Joash reached out and pulled her to him, whispering dangerously in her ear. "What they were going to do was not a whole lot different. How do you know what your life might have been like with this other man? And my horse has proved herself. You on the other hand will have to earn my trust."

Keturah felt something hot rise within her and ached to strike him. She hissed in his ear, "At least I don't attempt to steal things that aren't mine. You didn't do anything to earn what you got." Her cheeks blazed with heat, and she held her fists clenched to her side.

His jaw twitched. "There wasn't a choice. No one was going to break their vow to give us wives and what would the rest of us have done?"

Keturah's heart beat unsteadily, as she looked at him. "And yet, you might've done the honorable thing. We all have a choice."

Joash looked annoyed. "Other tribes said the Lord wouldn't want the Benjamite clan to die out. They encouraged it."

"And you believed this was of the Lord?" Her lips parted in disbelief. "You couldn't trust him to do something for the tribe? Or wait for his truth?"

He shook his head. "Not when they agreed."

She turned from him, looking out over the hills. "But, it was wrong, and you know it. And you knew all along it wasn't the right thing to do?"

He let out a sound. "What is *wrong*, anyway? And for that matter what is truth? How's anyone to know? The Lord has never given me answers."

Keturah looked shocked. He didn't believe in the Lord? And he was going to marry her? Something struck her deep inside, and she felt as if she were going to be sick. Hadn't she been praying? Would this truly be Adonai's will for her? "The Lord will show you truth if you ask and will answer your prayers."

She refused to look at him and turned away. "And whether you choose to believe him or not, someday you'll have to answer to him for what you've done."

He swung her back around to face him and scowled. "And where's your Lord, now?" His eyes sought hers. "Is this his answer to your careful prayer?"

Her dark hair had come loose about her shoulders, and she pushed it behind her, eyes flashing, ready to respond. How dare he speak to her about prayer?

He took by the wrists. "Tell me. I'd like to know."

But when she met his hardened eyes, and tried to pull herself away from his grip, she wondered what answer she *could* give him. What was she doing in this place so far from home on her way to Bethel to become this man's wife, when she so faithfully prayed for years for a life in Shiloh with her family? She suddenly felt confused. Why would the Lord allow something like this to happen? And then, she realized she had nothing to say. Tears flooded her eyes and dropped down her cheeks, as she looked up at him. It was all she could do.

He was about to say something, but instead, his mouth came close to hers, and it seemed as if he would kiss her. But, Keturah knew this couldn't happen. She suspected if it did, for this man, he wouldn't take it lightly, and there would most likely be no turning back.

She tensed, her dark eyes suddenly fearful, and struggled to pull away from him, but was unable to move.

He looked closely at her, and then something in his expression changed. He suddenly pushed her away, frowning.

"Get back on the horse." There was a troubled look in his eyes. "There's more riding to do."

Keturah's head ached, and she drew her hand up to her temples. She couldn't think. If there were only a way to escape, she'd do it. But, her legs wobbled beneath her, and every bone in her body ached. There was nothing she could do. No way out.

When she couldn't get on the horse on her own, he lifted her onto it and got up behind her, and they were on their way.

*****

"How long must I wrestle with my thoughts and day after day have sorrow in my heart? How long will my enemy triumph over me?" Psalm 13:2 King James's Version

Chapter 13

They'd been on the horse for a night and part of a day. Keturah's legs were cramped and aching, and she wished they'd stop to rest soon.

It was midday, and they were beginning to see some signs of life, valleys with some greenery and a couple trees dotting a small creek. The sun was at full strength and beat down on them, as the horse plodded slowly along. They found a spring a couple miles back, where the large animal was replenished enough to continue.

Keturah supposed they'd come upon the camp Joash spoke of very soon. Maybe she'd see Tirzah. She was hoping the soldiers would meet up to band together for protection. She might find her friend in the mix of them.

She scoured the horizon, but still didn't see any sign of other tribesmen in the hills, only the hot, baked earth with an occasional shrub or small tree line against a set of rocky terrain. She sighed, realizing she was getting further and further from Shiloh.

She reached out and touched the horse's black, thick mane. It was dusty and matted and coarse. She tried separating the strands with her fingers, something to keep her mind off what was happening.

Joash put his hand on her shoulder as they rode further down the trail. "You didn't tell me your name?" He leaned closer to her.

When she didn't answer and pulled back from him, he prodded her gently. "I can let your father know where you are."

She looked up at him, and her brow lifted slightly at his admission. "It's Keturah."

"Hmm, fragrant flower." He breathed in her ear. "When you were in the vineyards, you smelled like them."

She didn't answer him.

He tightened his grasp around her, not saying more.

They rode on without talking until close to sundown. Then, Joash pointed out. "Up ahead, we'll stop. The others will be there."

***

Joash reined in the tired horse. "Whoa." They drew to a halt in front of a large area near a spring where the soldiers from his company were gathered, tethering and watering their animals. The women there were setting up the tents. Many of them looked as if they'd been crying. Keturah didn't see anyone she knew.

Joash got off the horse and pulled it to a watering hole to drink.

When the horse bent his neck down, Keturah began to slide forward. She strained to hold herself on the large animal, grabbing its mane. She started slipping over the top of the horse.

Joash eyed her curiously and then laughed as if he found her situation humorous. He didn't move, watching to see what she'd do.

She ignored him, pushing on the sides of the horse. It took all her strength to stay on, but she wouldn't give Joash the satisfaction of asking for his help.

He smiled and moved to her before she fell, lifting her off and setting her aside.

And then he snorted. "Ha! It's what I tried to tell my father about women, and why I didn't want to be troubled with them."

She brushed the horsehair off her and turned away from him. She hadn't asked to be with him either. "Then, take me back." She spoke quietly. "Because, I don't want to be with you."

He laughed again behind her, but she didn't turn around.

His voice lowered, and she could barely hear him. "I'll not waste my horse on another trip to Shiloh."

She looked across the camp as far as she could see. Tents littered a craggy field that stretched a great distance, hundreds of them. She crinkled her nose at the smell of smoke from fires and the sweat of soldiers and their horses. The echoes of cries carried through the camp, while the men went dutifully about their tasks.

Her eyes moistened at the sight of a young woman, sitting next to a tent nearby holding her knees and rocking back and forth, murmuring quiet mournful sounds. She wanted to go to the woman to comfort her, but Joash took her arm and pulled her along.

Keturah scanned the path, looking for Tirzah, but didn't see her. "Could I see if I can find my friend?"

He shook his head. "We've no time for that."

Keturah didn't answer, but her brows furrowed, and she yanked her arm away from him.

He shrugged and pulled the horse beside a crude path to look for traders, guiding her to walk next to him. While he was making deals with the men there, Keturah's eyes were peeled for Tirzah. She assumed her friend was in the crowd, but with two hundred men and about the same number of women, it was difficult to tell.

Joash took her hand and pulled her along, his horse laden with supplies for the trip home. They walked up and down the rows.

"Daniel!" He called out to another man on the trail. He strode down the path until the two friends met, and they shook hands heartily.

Keturah stood back, eying them both distastefully. Daniel had a full beard and wide set eyes and was almost as tall as Joash. She noticed that most of the men from the tribe of Benjamin were tall, all warriors that had been in the desert.

When Daniel looked over at Keturah, his expression was one of concern. She could tell by his eyes that he was a more compassionate man than Joash. "So, she's the one you're bringing home." He lifted an eyebrow. "I pity her."

Joash gave his friend a nonchalant nod. "She'll be fine…if she learns to hold that tongue of hers."

Keturah didn't look at either of them, but instead stared at the hillside, trying to see the Ephraimite country where Shiloh was, but couldn't make out anything.

Daniel shook his head. "She's pretty."

Joash didn't say anything, but started unpacking the tent from the back of his horse.

Then he gestured for Keturah to sit, while he started putting up the tent. "We'll camp in this place."

She was surprised he wasn't having her do the work, but didn't complain. She was tired, so sat down on a mat he put out for her, watching him and Daniel set up the small makeshift place for them to lie down in.

Daniel motioned to his own tent. "If you wait inside, it'll be cooler in the shade. Ruth is in there. Although, she doesn't talk much."

Keturah gave him a stony look. "I can't imagine why." The tone of her voice was dry.

Joash looked annoyed at first. Then, he shook his head, and he got a lazy smile, watching her with interest. "She gives her opinions freely, so be careful what you say to her."

Keturah didn't answer, seeing how Joash seemed to enjoy making fun of her. She thought about the changes in her since she'd met him. He seemed to bring out the worst in her. She'd mostly been the obedient one in her home, meekly accepting what her parents wanted and dutifully carrying out any tasks set before her. But, with him, she felt as if she were on the defense and not able to hold back her thoughts.

Daniel shrugged. "At least you know what she's thinking."

"Yes, but she'll be setting up the tents, if she speaks too freely. I don't appreciate doing women's work."

Keturah rolled her eyes. She got up and went to the tent, not wanting to hear what they had to say. She ducked under the flap and went to the young woman sitting quietly inside.

"Ruth?" She eyed the pretty girl with long brown hair tied in a braid. Flowers left over from the festival were still dotting the length of it.

The young woman looked sad.

Keturah went over to her and put her arm around her. "It'll be all right. You'll see. He doesn't seem so bad."

Ruth looked up at her with large, brown eyes.

Keturah's heart went out to the young woman. She reached out and put her arms around her. "What's he done to you?"

Ruth blushed and spoke quietly. "Nothing. He said it is my choice whether I wish to be his wife or not. He wants to me to see his land and possessions first. And meet his family."

Keturah eyed Daniel curiously outside the tent. "Well, then, it's good for you. It seems he's not so bad." She patted Ruth's knee.

Ruth smiled. "I agree." And then her eyes were somber again. "But, I've never left Shiloh."

Keturah looked down. "Yes. I want to go back. But, we're so far away, and I don't believe the man I'm with will be as kind as Daniel. I'm sure I don't have a choice as to whether to marry or not."

Ruth put out her hand to take Keturah's. "I should be thankful." She lowered her voice to a whisper. "But, maybe you'll find a way."

Keturah sighed. She looked out toward the doorway of the tent. "He hasn't let me alone since we left Shiloh, and I wouldn't know how to get back if he did." She didn't want to think about it. She brushed some dirt from her tunic, realizing how dusty she'd become. "You haven't spoken to him?"

Ruth shook her head. "Hardly. I've been so distraught without my family."

"Well, none of them deserve anything for what they did." Keturah gave her a rueful look.

Ruth smiled. "But, maybe since Daniel's redeemed himself, I will speak to him."

Keturah shrugged. "At least he's given you a choice."

Ruth nodded. "Yes. It gives me hope."

***

Daniel looked surprised to see Ruth come out of the tent with Keturah.

Keturah went to sit back on the mat. She watched as Ruth went to Daniel and whispered something in his ear. Daniel smiled, as she sat down next to him to watch him work.

Keturah stared at them, almost enviously. Regardless of the way things were, Daniel was treating her considerately.

Joash stopped working and looked at Keturah. "What did you say to her?"

Keturah gave him an irksome stare. "I didn't have to say anything. He's a good man."

Joash shrugged, continuing with his work. "Would you like to finish the tent? Maybe you need something to do."

She didn't answer.

Shortly afterward, there was a shout that rang out through the camp. Joash went to speak with one of the men going from tent to tent, relaying information.

Keturah tried to listen, but couldn't hear what they were saying. She wished she were closer, but didn't want to appear as if she cared, so she stayed where she was.

She watched as Joash listened intently to the man. Then, they shook hands when they finished talking, and Joash turned. He strode back to her, his steps long and confident.

He had a pleased look on his face, when he reached her.

He leaned down and stroked her hair. "You were wrong, my fragrant flower." And then, he went back to his work.

Keturah gave him a look that could have withered a cypress tree. Whatever it was that was said, it made her feel very uneasy. She didn't like how he seemed so self-assured about it.

She wanted to hear what he learned. "About what?" Her face was flushed. "What did he say?"

Joash kept his back to her, but she could imagine the gratified look on his face. "Your people made a decision not to retaliate. Or to come for their daughters."

A breath caught in her throat. "But, that's wrong." She stared at him. "My father wouldn't do that. He'll be here."

He looked back at her with an amused expression and grinned. "He's not coming, and neither are the rest of your people. They understand our position and aren't going to deny their daughters the riches they'll inherit." His dark green eyes sparkled. "They understand we're brothers and family and that in doing this, they'll preserve the twelve tribes."

Keturah wished so badly she had a way of getting back at him and taking the arrogant smirk from his face.

But, she sat there not speaking, sick inside, while she watched the sun going down over the horizon. A terrible feeling of trepidation fell over her as he put up the last of the shelter.

When he was finished, he took her hand. "Come. We'll see a priest, now. This day, you'll become my wife."

***

Keturah wiped silent tears that fell down her cheeks in a continuous stream, while Joash slept soundly next to her, with his arm tightly about her waist. She felt as if the Lord had abandoned her. He seemed to have shut her out and left her to her own defenses in this dry wilderness. Every prayer she'd prayed about Shiloh and her friends and family, went unanswered and ignored. Everything, she'd hope for and believed in, seemed to be part of a huge lie.

The result of her prayers never included a man like Joash, or anyone resembling him. He was nothing like she imagined a husband to be, far from what she'd ever dreamed of.

A New Dance

She couldn't believe the ruse of it all, a way to get around the vow they'd taken before the Lord against the Benjamites. How could the Israelites think they were fooling the Almighty? Did they not know the Holy One could see through it all?

She wiped more tears and tried to pull off the strong arm that was encircling her waist, but could not.

This was her husband now, in the eyes of the Lord and there was no way out, nothing she could do to change things. And the people of Shiloh supported it. Her father, mother and brothers, they all betrayed her.

She gulped back a sob, wishing to die.

A sliver of moonlight fell over her husband's sleeping figure. She studied him while he slept, her eyes solemn. He was nothing like Hiram, unsympathetic, caring little for the way he treated her.

She prayed. "Why Lord, have you allowed this? What did I do to deserve such a thing?"

The smell of the goat-haired tent and smoke from the fire outside was strong in the air, and a cloud set upon the moon, as darkness fell over the small space she and Joash occupied. She thought she heard a low growl in the distance and shivered.

The Lord was supplying no answers tonight. How she could remain faithful to this Maker of hers, one who didn't feel very reliable? But, she knew she needed to. He was all she had.

***

"Joash." Keturah's voice was a whisper. She shook his arm.

He turned in the dark, morning hours. His eyes opened, and he reached for her.

"No, listen." She shivered, a chill going down her spine.

He sat up when a low, throaty growl occupied the area outside their tent. He put his fingers to his lips, signaling for her to keep silent and stay where she was. He got up and crept to the doorway, slipping out and leaving her there alone.

She pulled the furs tighter around her and tried to listen for more sounds but heard none at first. She was frozen in her spot, ready to bolt if necessary.

Then, a loud twang of a string and a thud echoed the cool morning air, along with the sound of something heavy dropping to the ground.

Joash came back in the tent after a few minutes and took her hand. He had a self-satisfied expression on his face. He pulled her outside. "We'll have meat." He pointed to a bear, which lay on the ground within feet of the tent. It wasn't breathing and had a wound to its head.

Keturah stared at it open-mouthed. She stepped behind him watching the animal to make sure it wouldn't get back up. "It's dead?"

He laughed. "Would I have brought you to see it, if it wasn't?" He eyed her curiously.

She backed away, keeping one eye on the bear and one on him. "I need to wash up and make breakfast."

"I'll care for this animal. Since it's still early, I'll finish before the caravan's ready to go again."

She didn't respond.

His eyes went to her face, and he reached out and touched the area under her eyes. "You didn't sleep well?"

She looked at him incredulous and pushed his hand away. "Of course not." She bristled. "And if you don't understand why, then you're worse than I thought."

He regarded her with an indifferent look. "Whether you agreed with this arrangement or not, Keturah, you're my wife, now. There's nothing you can do to change that."

She turned to the campfire, and began to stoke the flames with a stick, not answering.

He shrugged. "Suit yourself. It matters little to me." He gave her an indifferent look. "I only wanted a child."

Her mouth opened, and she stared at him, wondering what kind of person would say such a thing. She set the stick on the rocks that encircled the fire and sat down. Grabbing a wooden bowl of lentils, she began mashing them together in it. The man didn't seem to have a care for anyone but himself. What would her life be like with such a person?

He went over to the bear and knelt down by it, taking out his dagger and slicing into it. He carefully cut off the fur and pieces of meat from it, throwing them onto a wooden bowl by the fire. "Cook it. We'll eat before we leave, and I'll give the rest to the others. It'll not keep on the trail."

She sighed. "I need a sharpened stick to put them on."

She started pressing the lentil cakes together and placing them on a bronze dish near the edge of the fire. She'd have to get to the bear meat later.

***

Two more days on the trail. Keturah was tired.

She looked at Joash out of the corner of her eye, as he rose to bring her his empty plate. "Here, clean it."

She took it from him, her eyes darkening. With him, she felt more of a slave than a wife. If he only treated her, the way Daniel treated Ruth, it might not have been so bad.

He sat back down watching her with an expression of interest. "At one time, I had women conniving to get my attention and hopeful for marriage. And now, I have a wife who can't stand the sight of me."

"I wonder why." She muttered it under her breath. She looked perturbed. "So, why didn't you take one of them when you had the chance? Surely, it would've been better for someone like you, to have a woman who worshipped the path you walked on."

He didn't say anything at first, but then he reached out and took her hand, raising it to his lips and pressing his mouth against it, a churlish smile spreading across his face. "But, I didn't want them. I liked that passion I saw in your dance." His dark green eyes glittered, and his voice grew husky and deep. "Not what my mother would have looked for."

Keturah pulled back her hand, unnerved. She turned back to the fire, indignant. Why did he say this? Her dance was for the Lord, and was meant to be beautiful. He made her feel as if it were impure.

What could she have done differently to keep from ending up in this place with him? She couldn't stop the thoughts racing through her mind. She wished she wouldn't have danced in the vineyards that day. There was a heavy feeling in her chest and a deep sadness tearing at her insides, knowing there was no way out of it, nothing she could do. Her marriage to him ended any other dream she had. *****

"And my people shall dwell in a peaceable habitation, and in sure dwellings, and in quiet resting places." Isaiah 32:18 King James's Version

Chapter 14

The caravan of riders took different directions at a fork in the road. Daniel's cart continued on the path, as Joash veered off in a different direction. Keturah felt a lonely jolt in her chest, as she watched Ruth's tiny figure fade into the distance. She'd never found Tirzah in the crowd, and was losing Ruth as well.

Keturah eyed the hillside and the valley where Bethel lay, which sprawled out in all directions below.

"It's your home, now." Joash pointed to the town ahead. "Our place is just inside the city walls. My family will be waiting."

She didn't respond, but looked at the massive stonewall that snaked its way around the mud-brick homes in the town.

She was prepared to hate Bethel. But, after seeing it, understood why those who lived there had chosen to build a city in such an area. Lovely, flower-filled vineyards covered the side of the hills and bubbling springs flowed from the ground near to where they stopped to water their animals. The air was free of dust, and the sky behind was one of the clearest blue Keturah had ever seen.

It was the first thing that lightened Keturah's heart since she left Shiloh.

Joash got down beside the horse and walked. He took the reigns and led the animal down the path, as she rode in silence.

***

Keturah's mouth opened slightly as they neared a massive stone gateway made of large, round boulders cemented together with mud. It was set on the side of the hill bordering the city.

Vineyards encircled the property, hanging with lush, purple grapes. Hundreds of sheep and goats roamed within a huge gated area, making low quiet cries, separated by an area that housed three camels. Her breath practically caught in her throat at the size of the solid rock hewn home.

She reached up laying her hand on her chest.

He looked up at her, as if pleased with her reaction. "I see you like it."

She dropped her eyes, not answering.

"My mother, father and sister are ahead. They were of the few who weren't here when the massacre happened." He clicked the side of his horse with his heel. "I warned them, and they got out in time."

She turned to see three people standing inside the courtyard as Joash brought the horse she was riding, through the rectangular gate.

His family was all dressed in clean, well-made cloth, tightly woven in bright colors. His mother and sister both wore simple gold jewels around their neck and arms and soft leather ties around their small waists. She eyed them warily.

If his family were anything like him, she didn't know if she could bear it. Her innards were in knots at the thought of meeting them. Would they treat her kindly?

Joash lifted Keturah from the horse. She was unsteady on her feet as she held his arm, staring at the dry, cracked earth beneath her. She hadn't had a chance to clean herself along the way, so felt dusty and hot, and her lips were parched. Her hair had a gritty feel, and she was sure it was unkempt looking. What would they think of her? Did they know the extent of what their son had done?

Joash's mother immediately came rushing up and cupped Keturah's face in her hands. "Oh, my. How tired you must be, daughter." Her manner was so different from her son, so kind and full of hospitality. How could this compassionate woman have raised such a man?

Keturah nodded. She said nothing, regarding Joash's mother with a mixture of sadness and confusion. She pushed her hair back behind her and willed herself to still her trembling body.

"Please. Call me, Mary." Joash's mother motioned to the young woman standing next to her. "This is Nissa. Our daughter. She's mute, but understands what we say."

Nissa smiled, and Keturah could sense kindness emanating from her. She immediately knew she'd have an ally in Joash's sister.

Mary studied Keturah's face, and the wrinkles around her eyes drew upward. "You're a sweet girl. I can tell. Isn't she, Joash?" She turned to her son.

Joash laughed, eying Keturah with a wry grin. He reached out, pushing her hair back from her face.

Keturah took her hand away from his arm and brushed him away. A flame rose in her cheeks, and she turned from him.

"Don't let her deceive you." He patted the side of his horse. "Now, this one here is the sweet one."

His mother scolded him. "Joash. Leave her be." Her brows drew together. "What've you done?"

Keturah looked back up at him, her eyes daggers.

He laughed, turning to his father who was regarding him silently. Then, he snorted and let out a breath. "Take her to the house with Nissa to get her settled. She needs a bath and clean clothes. Nissa's should fit her."

His mother took Keturah's arm. "What's your name?"

Joash answered for her. "Keturah. From Shiloh."

"I can answer myself." Keturah bristled, and her eyes narrowed.

"See. The temper." He laughed again.

"Joash!" His mother admonished him. "Enough."

His father spoke for the first time. He looked at Keturah, turning away from his son. He adjusted the sides of his striped purple and white robe and bent his head to her. "I'm sorry for the circumstances that brought you to this place." His expression was somber. "This act was not condoned by Joash's mother or I, or we believe by the Lord, for that matter. I only hope you'll find our home welcoming. My name's Simeon."

Keturah nodded. She took a couple steps toward Joash's father and stopped in front of him, raising the hem of his sleeve to her lips to kiss it. "You're my father now. Your kind words strengthen me. I'll do my best to please you."

Simeon smiled and seemed won over right away by her. He took Keturah's hand in his. "And I you."

She smiled at Simeon. Then, she took Joash's mother's hand and walked with the women to the house, turning once to send Joash a dark look.

Joash just smiled, taking the reigns of his horse and patting its side tenderly.

Keturah stared at him with a look of ire. He could have his sweet animal, she thought. If by now, he didn't know why she treated him the way she did, then she wanted no part of him.

She noticed Simeon's bothered expression, when he turned to his son. They were still near the gate arguing as she left the courtyard and went into the house.

Maybe here, Joash wouldn't get away with being so unkind.

She hoped so, anyway. At least she'd have support and encouragement with these people who were his family.

*****

"And let us arise and go up to Bethel; and I will make there an altar unto God, who answered me in the day of my distress and was with me in the way which I went." Genesis 35:3 King James's Version

Chapter 15

The next morning, Keturah woke early. She washed and dressed in a clean tan-colored tunic Nissa had given her. She fingered the fringed edge with the ribbon of blue along the bottom and on the sleeves. It was simple, and a bit work worn, but a welcome relief from the dusty one she'd worn on the trail. It felt good to bathe at the spring.

When she finished braiding her hair, she quietly slipped out of the tiny room leaving Joash asleep. She tiptoed across the hard clay floor strewn with sweet-smelling straw beneath her feet, and raised the latch of the heavy, wooden door in the front room and pushed it open.

Sunrays washed over her, and she turned her face to the light, drinking in the warm morning air. She closed the door behind her and walked out into the courtyard and through the stone gate. Sheep were in a pen, bleating and a couple donkeys brayed from inside a cave stable built into a rocky wall near the house. There was the crackle of fire and a faint smell of smoke in the air. She walked alongside the outer wall of the courtyard and came to a stone altar. Joash's father was kneeling in front of it in prayer, his lips moving and head bent.

Keturah turned to go back, when she thought she might be intruding.

"No, come here, daughter." Simeon called to her from behind.

"I'm sorry." A look of concern crossed Keturah's face. "I didn't mean to disturb you."

"No, you didn't." Simeon motioned to her. "Let's talk and then pray together. I'd like to know more about you."

Keturah went and knelt beside him. She eyed the tall, stone altar with a fire burning on top. The flame flickered high and crackled loudly.

Simeon touched the sleeve of her tunic. "Nissa gave it to you?"

She nodded then pointed to the embroidery along the sleeves. "It's well made."

Simeon smiled. "My wife's good with cloth. She put a blue ribbon on this one. Do you understand what this means?"

"To not forget the commandments. And I'll try my best to remember them. I pray to the Lord every day."

He nodded and sighed. "You're a good girl."

And then, the lines in Simeon's face deepened. His eyes met hers, as if he wanted to ask her some things. "My son has a lot to learn. Did he treat you all right along the trail?"

Keturah shrugged. "Well enough." But, her heart didn't agree.

Simeon looked out over the hills. "The life of a soldier is rough. He's seen a lot of death and lost friends. The young men aren't following the Lord, as they should."

"Did he ever follow the Lord?"

Simeon didn't answer at first. Then, his voice grew pensive. "When he was young. Life's changed him."

Keturah didn't say anything.

Simeon looked grim. "I guess I should've watched him more closely when he was a child. He grew tall very quickly and was always strong. The other children admired him, maybe a little too much. He's always been confident and self-assured."

Keturah could think of other things he was also, but didn't say. Instead, she spoke quietly. "I'm not sure he even wanted a wife."

Simeon squeezed her hand. "I don't understand, as he has a lovely one." Then, he patted her shoulder.

Keturah felt tears welling up in her eyes and wiped them away. "I'm obligated to remain here with him, so I'll do my best."

Simeon rested his hand on her shoulder. And then he let go, looking up at the stone altar. "Keep asking the Lord for his help." He had a soft expression on his face. "It can't be easy, the way this happened, but if you try to show respect to my son, as difficult as it may seem, maybe he'll see things different. I think it's what the Lord would want."

Keturah put her hand to the gold necklace her father had given her and fingered it gently. "I've been obedient with my parents and with others, but with Joash…" She was at a loss for words. "With him, it's not the same. He's difficult."

Simeon eyes were warm. "Then, keep praying."

Keturah nodded. "And have faith that the Lord can do what I can't."

"Yes." Simeon agreed. Then, he closed his eyes and bent his head.

Keturah did the same, praying to the Lord for mercy and his peace. The sweet smelling incense rose up around them and felt like part of her prayer, lifting to the heavens. She breathed in its deep, rich scent.

The air was balmy and the morning quiet, save for the soft snapping sounds of the fire and the bird's gentle songs above them. Although she still had a hard time seeing this as her home, Keturah felt the peace around her this morning.

But, before she was able to finish her prayers, she was interrupted. There was a sound behind her, and she turned.

"Get up!" Joash grabbed her arm and yanked her to her feet. His eyes were narrowed, and his jaw was firmly set. "Why didn't you tell me you left?"

She pulled away from him. "You were asleep." There was a snappish tone to her voice. "And I'm with your father."

Simeon stood up. "Joash, she meant no harm."

Joash looked annoyed and put out his hand. "Stay out of it, father. It's not your place."

Simeon shot his son a look of warning.

Keturah gave Joash a shove. "Stop! Please. You can't treat your father like this."

He took her arm, giving her an annoyed look. "Don't say more. We've work to do."

She let out a breath, her eyes meeting his. "But, I wasn't finished." Keturah choked back a sob. "I have to pray."

He began to pull her from the altar. "For what? To try and leave this place?"

Keturah dug her feet into the earth. "No. You don't understand. I'm not going to, as we're married now. But, I need to pray. You can't take this from me." Her brows drew to a frown, and she pulled back from him. Her heart felt suddenly faint.

He let go of her arm, as he looked from his father to her, and then shook his head, clearly aggravated. He eyed the altar distastefully. "Fine. Pray, what good it will do you. But, be quick, or I'll drag you out of here next time."

And then he turned and stalked off, leaving Keturah with Simeon.

She slumped down at the base of the altar. A pain stabbed her chest. It wasn't at all what she pictured marriage to be. Why had the

Lord allowed this to happen? Joash was impossible. She'd no idea how to deal with him.

"See. What I told you is true. Everything that's obedient in me is gone when he's around. I feel as if I've no control over it."

Simeon shook his head. "He's not an easy man. And it was right to stand up for your time with the Lord. You weren't unkind."

Keturah wiped tears from her eyes. There was a small light in them when she looked at him. "Thank you, Simeon. I'll keep praying. And I'm sorry if I disrespected your son."

"The Lord answered my prayers in sending you to Joash. Adonai will make things right."

She looked puzzled. "Your prayers?"

"Yes, I am sure it's the reason you're here, for my son. But, I'm sorry you're paying such a high price for his sin."

She looked over at the house and then at Simeon. "I don't understand. But, it gives me hope to know you love the Lord, too. And that he can change things."

He nodded. "You're a wise daughter."

"Thank you, Simeon."

Then, she bent her head to finish her morning prayers.

*****

"Before that time there were no wages for people or hire for animals. No one could go about their business safely because of their enemies, since I had turned everyone against their neighbor." Zechariah 8:10 King James's Version

Chapter 16

In the courtyard, after the family had eaten the morning meal, Joash took Keturah's hand and pulled her from a wooden bench in the main room of the house. "I've business in the city. You're going with me."

She stared at the open doorway that led to the courtyard and then back at him. "But, we just got here."

He took a woven basket from the shelf and thrust it into her hand, his eyes narrowing. The look on his face told her he wasn't in the mood to listen to her protest, so she fell silent. She'd learned in the few days she'd been around him, he wasn't accustomed to answering to anyone or being challenged and didn't appreciate having to explain himself to her.

She lifted her eyes upward, directing a quick prayer to the Lord. Keep me from his temper. Show me what you want, and what to say.

He put his hand on her back as he went with her outside the courtyard. He set her on top of a donkey and went to the front, grabbing the harness and rope and pulling it in the direction of the city.

The cart rattled and bumped over the dusty path, and she looked behind her. Nissa and his parents were nowhere in sight.

She rode in silence, while Joash led the mule down the city streets.

As they made entrance deeper into the heart of the city, a feeling of trepidation suddenly ran through her. Her mother warned her of the wickedness of the people of the streets deep in the heart of the city.

The path began to narrow, and people were thick around them. Flutes piped out eerie tunes, and drummers beat hides stretched taut with sinewy ropes, thumping in unison to the clomping of donkey's hooves.

A jeweled, veiled woman pushed a platter of sweet food at Keturah's hands, the kohl under the woman's eyes thick and catlike and her words slurred. "For a Shekel, taste the magic in the pastries." She smiled, staggering toward the cart. She slid her leg out of a slit in her tunic, eying Joash slyly.

Keturah turned her head and cast her eyes at the ground. She felt sick inside, knowing how her parents would have never exposed her to these people so far from the safety of her home.

There was a heavy scent of incense and perfume in the air, intermixed with the sweat and grime of traders. Wolfish howls rang out as the venders yelled their prices and animals were herded into pens next to them. A fight broke out not far from them, and two men stumbled past, drunk on wine.

When the cart drew to a halt, she turned to the sound of men's bantering with each other. Joash looked up at her and his eyes grazed hers, a spark in them.

Her cheeks felt hot, and she turned away. She could hear his laugh blending with the other men.

"She's the one from Shiloh."

One of the men let out a snort. "Joash caught a prize." And all the men laughed with him.

Keturah wouldn't lift her eyes to them, a faint feeling coming over her.

One of the men grazed the side of her tunic with his hand, and she tensed, pulling back and pushing him away. His leering eyes raked over her boldly.

She turned to Joash who wore an amused grin. Why'd he allow such a thing? What kind of a man was she betrothed to?

She pulled her wrap tighter and looked away, her heart pounding in her chest.

"She doesn't look as if she belongs with the lot of us." There was a crude, interested tone in one of the men's voice. He was standing next to her.

She shuddered, closing her eyes, her lashes fanning against her cheeks.

Joash shrugged. "She'll have to get used to it, as she's my wife now."

She directed an embittered stare his way, biting back a retort.

The man closest to him watched her curiously, something calculating lighting his eye. His skin was rough and tanned, and a scar mirrored the one that ran down Joash's cheek. "I get the impression there's a bit of a fire in her. Careful, Joash, or you just might get burned."

Joash's dark green eyes narrowed, assessing Keturah coldly at first. And then with a cynical look, he threw back his head and laughed. "Ha! Show me any woman, and they're sure to possess a bite at some point."

Keturah's faced flamed, and she looked away again.

All the men began to laugh.

Luckily, their attention turned from her, when they loaded wares into the back of the cart and exchanged coins. As they took swigs of wine from cups, they spoke in low tones about the market deals they were making.

Keturah thought the worst was over, until the man nearest her suddenly reached out and caught her about the waist, his eyes trained on her. "Joash should do the hospitable thing." He pulled her from the mule and yanked her against him. "And be willing to share what he has."

Keturah pushed the smelly, drunken man from her, shrinking from the others who nodded at his suggestion, suddenly staring at her hungrily like a pack of wolves encircling her.

Joash only chuckled with them, as if it was a game and she was a token.

She was shoved into the hands of one of the men who sifted her hair in his hand. And then she was pushed around the group as they continued howling and jesting with her.

Tears began to flood her eyes. And as much as she detested and despised Joash, she instinctively sought him out to help her.

Through blurred vision and strands of hair having fallen into disarray about her face, she caught his eye and broke free, tearing through the men and into his arms. Her breath came in gulps, and she held tightly to him weeping. "Take me out of here, please." Her voice was a whisper. Her eyes met his. "I want to go. With you."

There was an odd mixture in his expression she couldn't quite read.

She repeated herself. "Please, I don't want to be here."

Joash shrugged, seemingly noncommittal. He put up his hand. "Leave her alone."

"Here." He threw them a moneybag. "Get more to drink."

The men began to laugh again, until one of them let out a wounded sound. "Wine for her? Not exactly a fair trade."

Another man with dark whiskers, scowled. "He's right. Joash should show us hospitality. The wine's little consolation for that beauty of his. We can get more money and drink any day."

Keturah felt sick and weak, as if her knees were going to buckle from under her. She clung to Joash tighter. "Please."

He suddenly lifted his hand to her hair and smoothed it behind her.

He stared at the men and put his arm out to them, motioning for them to stop. He got a dangerous gleam in his eye and looked around. "Don't, unless you want to fight." Then he smiled at the possibility of a brawl.

The man who took her from the horse stepped back, chuckling nervously. "But, Joash, it's the hospitable thing to do."

Joash scowled. He put Keturah behind him, taking a dagger from his side and gripping it tightly in his hand. "But I said, you must fight for it."

The man put up his hand and wiped his forehead, which had begun to drip with sweat. "I didn't think it'd be a problem. But, I don't want a match with you or anyone else."

Joash shrugged. "A wise choice." He dipped his head, and then smiled unceremoniously. "And you're right to be this way. It'd be foolish to fight over any woman. It only leads to trouble."

The others nodded, breaking out into wide grins. They began clapping each other on the backs, laughing and drinking, turning away from him.

The man closest to him motioned to the cart. "You should get on the path. You shouldn't have brought her here, if you didn't want a scene."

Joash turned to Keturah, lifting a brow. He put her on the mule.

Then, the other man hit him on the arm and grinned. "She's pretty, but even so, I never thought I'd see you toting a wife around."

"I should've left her home, what good she's been." Joash scowled, and then he shrugged. "At least mother's quit bringing those simpering females to my table every night. I had just about enough of that."

The man with the scar roared with hilarity. "I think she is worth more than you believe." He tipped his head to the drunken men raising their cups in the air, one of them dumping it on his head. "A woman like this deserves more than those churlish wolves."

Keturah was seething inside. As if they weren't churlish wolves, themselves. She wiped the tears from her eyes and stiffened in her seat, staring coldly ahead when she felt Joash's eyes on her. She couldn't even bring herself to look at him. She just wanted to get back to the house safely.

After the two men shook hands, the wagon began moving, and she choked back a sob. Finally, they'd be getting out of this place. She never wanted to come here again.

She didn't feel completely safe, until they reached the edge of the city. She turned back more than once to make sure they weren't being followed.

Joash didn't seem to be affected by anything that had happened.

When they reached a turn in the road, he stopped the cart and looked at her. "Seems your Lord doesn't do a whole lot for you." His eyes glittered. "Even with all those prayers at that altar each day."

She stared at him, her eyes blazing. "My Lord had nothing to do with your low deeds. He wants good things for me. Something you know nothing about."

He threw back his head and laughed. "And you repay him by using that sharp tongue of yours toward your husband. He can't be that good, because you haven't learned anything from him."

Keturah replied dryly. "He kept me from those men. I'm sure *he* had more to do with it then you did."

He shrugged. "I could've given you to them."

She turned aside, feeling sick and said in a small voice. "But, you didn't."

He lifted a brow, grasping the reigns and turning his attention back to the road. He started on the path again, not looking back.

Keturah stared at him. What kind of man was she married to? How could she listen to Simeon's instruction and respect his son, when he dealt with her the way her did?

Despite his treatment of her, what he said disturbed her. He was right about her using her tongue as a weapon and not for good. One sin took no precedence over another with the Lord. And because of this, she was no better than he was.

Yet, despite her own sin, she bristled at the thought of ever being kind to him. How could she listen to a man as despicable he was?

She watched houses and fields of barley wheat pass by, and tears filled her eyes.

She wrestled with her thoughts of what she'd promised that morning at the altar. Did she stand behind her vows to others?

Joash's father, Simeon, seemed wise. Maybe if she'd listened to him, she might help Joash see who the Lord was. He'd never see the goodness of the Lord, unless someone showed him. She bowed her head in prayer, asking the Lord to help her.

As they neared Joash's home, thoughts kept entering her mind, and she knew God was prompting her to do something she didn't want to, something utterly detestable to her.

She felt a thick wall in her chest, and an edge to her fury so sharp she could barely breathe. Her heart rebelled against what she knew the Lord wanted.

How could he ask such a thing of her?

She sighed wearily, knowing she'd made the Lord her master, and she'd the choice to obey him or not. If she didn't do what the Lord prompted her to do, who was she serving, him? Or herself?

Tears filled her eyes, and she dropped her head, letting out a breath. Lord, she prayed, I'm your handmaid. Give me strength to serve you, not in the way I want, but in the way you desire. Help me remember, it is you I serve, not that detestable husband of mine.

She gritted her teeth, determined. The Lord was first in her heart. She'd do his will, and not be a prisoner to her own will, no matter how repulsive she felt his will was to her.

When Joash stopped the cart and lifted her down, she looked up at him, her eyes conveying her uncertainty.

He stood there, staring at her curiously, as if he wondered what she was about to do.

And then, while he watched, she reluctantly knelt down in front of him, stooping in the road. She reached out and begrudgingly lifted the dusty hem of his robe to her mouth, pressing it against her lips and kissing it. It was one of the most difficult things she'd ever done, as this man was one she considered despicable. But, it was something she knew the Lord had prompted her to do.

She felt tears falling from her eyes and watched them drop onto his feet. She wiped them away with a length of her hair stared at him. Her voice was a whisper. "I'm grateful for what you did today." She practically choked on her words. And she began to weep and kiss the hem of his robe again.

She felt Joash's arms around her, lifting her to her feet. He set her in front of him and pushed her hair back behind her. He began wiping the tears and dust from her cheek. He looked as if he'd been caught off guard and didn't know what to say.

Keturah lifted her hand to touch his face.

There was something gentle for a fleeting moment in his eyes, and he pulled her into his arms holding her there, pressing his face into her hair. "Keturah...I."

She pushed away from him, puzzled at his reaction.

And then he blinked. He suddenly tensed and cast her from him. The tender expression was gone, replaced by his familiar hard one. "Go, wash up. Mother will want you clean." He suddenly turned and walked away, leaving her standing next to the cart.

*****

"Hear me when I call, O God of my righteousness: thou hast enlarged me when I was in distress..." Psalm 4:1 King James Version

Chapter 17

Keturah led the mule to the gate and tied it to a post, then made her way to the spring to get water for washing. As she neared the bubbling brook next to the house, she sat down at its bank and put her head in her hands, holding back the tears threatening to spill. She let out a slow breath and looked up at the expanse of the sky.

What do you want, Lord? How can I bear this?

She leaned over and cupped her hands in the water, drawing it to her and washing her face. She filled the watering jar next to the bank and lifted it to her shoulder.

But, before she took a step, there was a rustle on the ground near her feet, and she looked down. When her eyes rested on a rock beside her, she froze. A large, golden-brown colored viper with dark markings on it was lifting its head, as if ready to strike.

Keturah drew in a slow breath. The water jar on her shoulder was heavy, but she didn't move. She was having difficulty steadying herself.

She prayed for the Lord's protection and care.

Then, suddenly there was a whirring sound behind her, but she couldn't look back to see what it was.

When the snake suddenly vaulted upward, she dropped the water jar and screamed, running from it. Joash was behind her. He started walking toward the spring.

She cried out when he headed in its direction. "No!"

When he walked past her, she grabbed his arm and tried to pull him back. "No! Don't go there! There's a snake!"

He turned and studied her closely. "But, it's dead."

And then, he suddenly looked amused. "And I'd think anyone in your place would be glad for that viper to kill me, so why do you care?"

She stared at him askew. "How can you say this? Glad? How would anyone feel glad for anyone else to die?"

He gave her an odd look, and then shrugged. "You evidently don't deal with the same people I do."

Keturah sputtered, heat going to her face. "Evidently, I don't. Before this, anyway."

He grinned, as if pleased by her reaction to his admission.

She wondered what was going through his mind. "But, why would anyone think this way?"

"You wouldn't understand." Then, he looked grim when he spoke. "But don't try to, either. You don't need to know anything about how I think or what I feel."

For the briefest of moments, she felt almost sorry for him. She reached out to him, but he pushed her hand back.

"But, I'm your wife. I should know my husband."

He looked down at the creek bed. His face seemed a mixture of emotion, and he turned from her. And then a darker look returned to his face. "Daniel was right when he said you were to be pitied."

He shoved her away and walked to the water's edge, bending down and took the viper by the back of its neck. He lifted it higher and carried it to a wooded area and tossed it in.

He washed his hands and then filled the water jar, lifting it, to carry back. "Come. Mother's waiting."

He reached out and touched the side of her face with his free hand, wiping dust from it. "And now, you've managed to get more dirt on yourself."

He put the jar down and touched a strand of her hair that fell over her shoulder. "Even with the dust, you're pretty. It's why they were fighting over you in the city."

Keturah questioned the strange look in his eyes. She stared at him, a frown on her brow. "You wouldn't have given me to them, would you?"

He looked at her as if unsure of what to say. He let go of the strand of hair he held in his hand.

Keturah stared at him.

His breath was weary. "Don't get ideas that I'm a better man than I am, because I'm not." His jawline tightened, and he let go of her. He lifted the jar back up.

"Joash?"

He backed away from her. His expression darkened.

Keturah knew it wouldn't do to ask him more.

78

"We need to get back."

Keturah walked beside him, occasionally stealing a glance at his grim profile and wondering what was beneath the mask he wore.

*****

"For jealousy is the rage of a man: therefore he will not spare in the day of vengeance." Proverbs 6:34 King James's Version

Chapter 18

The next morning, Joash's mother held out a water jar to Nissa. "Take Keturah and show her where the well is."

Nissa took the jar from her mother's hands, resting it on her shoulder, and clasped onto Keturah's hand.

Keturah took light steps alongside the young woman, wondering how they'd communicate when Nissa didn't speak. She eyed the girl curiously, feeling a sudden ache for her friend, Tirzah. She wished she'd seen Tirzah along the trail. She turned to study the girl who was now her sister.

Nissa had her brother's dark looks and the same greenish colored eyes.

She was definitely different from Joash in many ways, especially in demeanor, almost the opposite. Whereas he seemed self-assured with few manners, Nissa was very timid and unsure of herself, yet polite. And though he was tall and broad, she was slender and small. They presented a striking contrast to each other when they were together.

Nissa turned, smiling at Keturah. Her eyes were animated, as she pulled Keturah down the path and then let go of her arm to point ahead.

"It's there? You want me to carry it some of the way?"

Nissa shook her head, shifting the jar to her other side. She held it tight to her and smiled.

Keturah looked down the path. She could see women surrounding a well in the middle of the street. A few men stood to the side of the road, casually talking to each other.

"It's not far to walk. This is good."

Nissa agreed with a shake of her head, taking the jar to the well and setting it down next to the edge.

There were fewer women at this well than in Shiloh, and it was less animated. Only the Manassite women and the ones taken from Shiloh were there. Keturah noticed the absence of the children and older women as well. It all seemed very odd without the cries and laughter of the very young and the crinkling faces of the elderly. And it was apparent there were few close friends, by the quiet chatter and rare smiles.

Nissa pulled on the twine to raise the container from the bottom of the well, while Keturah watched.

Keturah suddenly felt a tug on her shoulder and turned.

A tall man, with a chalice of strong smelling drink in his hand had come from the road. He reached out and touched her hair. "I've not seen you here before. A gleam came to his eye."

She pulled away, her eyes narrowing. Were there any decent men in this city other than Joash's father? "Please...we have to go."

Nissa finished filling her jar and stood up to leave with Keturah. Her expression was wary and frightened at the same time.

The man stepped ahead of them and stood in their way. He took ahold of Keturah's arm. "Not just yet." His words came out in a snarl.

Nissa tried to push him off, but he knocked her to the ground as the water spilled out. She let out an injured sound.

"Watch it!" He put his hand on the back of Keturah's shoulder and drew her near.

"Stop!" She tried to push him away, but the man was stronger than she was, and she found herself being dragged toward the path, to where his camel was a few feet away. She looked around for someone to help, but found no one.

Then, she breathed a sigh of relief. Joash was coming down the road, his eyes dark as he took lengthy strides toward them. When he reached her, he quickly took hold of the man and shoved him backwards. Keturah cringed and moved away.

Joash growled menacingly at the man. "Do not touch her again, or you'll regret it. The woman is mine."

The other man suddenly looked like an old wineskin shrinking away.

Keturah backed further from them, letting out a sound. She gritted her teeth. His? He needed to learn a thing or two about her feelings. Maybe in marriage, she was, but not in any other way.

Joash looked at her and scowled. Then, he turned back to the man, again who had stumbled and fallen on the ground. "Never again. You hear?"

The man's eyes grew large as Joash towered over him. He put up his hands in a pleading gesture. "I didn't know who she was." He began to back away.

Joash's feet were planted widely apart, and he looked as if he would kill the guy. "Get out of here. And do it quickly."

Keturah shuddered. "He didn't do anything. Really."

Joash's glittering eyes rested on her, daring her to say more.

Keturah was silent. She bit her lower lip.

The man slunk away, taking the camel and hurriedly leading it down the path.

Nissa's eyes were wide, but she picked up her water jar and lifted it to her hip.

Joash grabbed Keturah's arm and pushed her ahead of him. "What did you do to have him react like that?" His eyes were hard and his voice a low growl.

Keturah cringed and drew back from him. She didn't answer.

Nissa put the jar down and went to her brother, tugging on his arm. She looked worried.

He shrugged her off. "Go home, Nissa. It's not your concern."

Keturah nodded to her. "Don't worry. Take the jar back. We'll come after you."

Nissa looked unsure.

"Please." Keturah tried to appear as confident as she could, to get Nissa to safety. There was no telling what her brother would do, if she got involved any further.

Nissa quietly took the jar in her hands and lifted it to her shoulder. Her face was pale, and she still seemed unsure, but turned reluctantly down the path toward the home.

Keturah whirled about, and pushed Joash's arm. "Why did you scare her like that? What were you thinking?"

Then, she stared back up at him. A dark rage simmered in Joash's eyes and the tightness in the lines of his mouth, and she backed away. She felt a sinking in the pit of her stomach. "I did nothing. I didn't even look at the man."

His eyes narrowed, and he scowled as he raked his eyes over her. "It isn't an accident when a man looks at a woman that way. You must have encouraged him in some way, so do not look at me as if you're innocent." He took her arm and began to drag her down the path toward their home.

Keturah tried pulling away from him. "Stop! What are you saying? That I caused this to happen?"

He let out a low laugh and stopped in his tracks, pulling her to him. "I know how women scheme for the favor of men and see no exception in you." He studied her face, as if he was looking for the guile he spoke of. "You think you're different?"

She looked up at him incredulous, her eyes widening. How could he say these things, when they weren't true?

She prayed for the right words to come. The Lord would tell her what to say.

She looked down, her cheeks burning. "I wouldn't dishonor my family or you by doing anything like this." She wiped at a tear that fell onto her cheek. She felt sick inside that he could think of her the way he did. "That man. He came to me when I wasn't looking. I tried to get away."

She choked on her words, as tears freely fell, and she wiped them away with her scarf. "Are all the men in this place, this way? I don't understand it. I don't understand you." She looked at him in disbelief. "I want nothing to do with any of it. I am innocent, even if you choose to not believe me." She covered her face with her hands.

He took her hands in his, drawing them away from her face and looked down at her. His narrowed eyes softened slightly. He took her by the arm with less force and began to lead her down the path. "Don't go near the men here."

She let out a breath. "But, I didn't. I wouldn't."

She stopped walking and looked up at him. She said the words she felt coming to her, but only in obedience to the Lord, as she knew this is what he wanted her to say. "My husband's the only one I desire." She reached up and touched his set jawline, just below the scar on his cheek and then lowered her hand to her side. "The Lord's given me to you. I don't know why. But, I wouldn't ever do anything like you say." She looked at him with tenderness.

And then she willed herself to smile and felt the pink growing in her cheeks as she spoke again. "And what man would come within a goat's length of me, when they learn you're my husband, anyway?"

Joash stared at her, as if seeing her for the first time. He didn't seem to know how to respond, as if he were caught off guard. He shoved her away from him. "Don't go anywhere without Nissa or my mother. We'll go home."

Keturah nodded and dusted off her tunic.

After she'd prayed, she believed the Lord stepped in and protected her. She realized at that moment, she was unable to do battle with this man, and would need to rely on the Lord's wisdom and goodness.

She moved to his side and walked next to him in silence on the path, in the direction of their home.

*****

"The Lord is my shepherd; I shall not want. He maketh me to lie down in green pastures: he leadeth me beside the still waters. He restoreth my soul: he leadeth me in the paths of righteousness for his name's sake." Psalm 23:1-3 King James Version

Chapter 19

Mary called for Nissa and Keturah to come into the courtyard.

Keturah finished what she was doing and made her way outside, through the open doorway. The sun was bright, and there was a light breeze.

Mary was standing a distance from a large vat filled with grapes not far from the doorway. She motioned to Keturah, pointing a the vat. "It's ready, if you'd like to help. It's Nissa's favorite job."

Nissa climbed over the edge of the large, round container filled with grapes and began to stomp on the small fruit with her bare feet. She let out a light laugh as the juice began to ooze from the dark berries.

Keturah smiled. "I'm coming. Just wait. Let me get my sandals off."

She went to the bench and untied the straps placing them beside her and washing her feet with water in the bowl next to the vat. At least she was beginning to warm to Joash's family. She hoped she might win their love, despite her husband.

When her feet were thoroughly clean, she lifted her legs over the edge and stepped in. The grapes squished under her feet. She slipped and quickly grasped hold of Nissa's arm. They both giggled.

Nissa laughed aloud, and then they let go, trampling on the grapes beneath the skirts they held up in their hands.

They drew an audience, as Mary and Simeon came nearer, smiles breaking out on their faces.

Keturah felt lighthearted and as if her family back home were surrounding her as she danced over the grapes. She nodded to Nissa. "Keep going."

The grapes in the bottom were getting flatter and juice was running over the tops of her feet.

Nissa grasped Keturah's arm to steady her. Her eyes sparkled as they worked together.

Keturah looked over at a movement near the fence where the horse and goats were kept, and her eyes met Joash's. He was looking at her as if intrigued, a half-smile on his face. He was handsome when he wasn't scowling, she thought. She wondered why he seemed to prefer it, instead.

Joash shook his head and went back to his work, brushing his horse and preparing it to ride. He talked softly to his horse, looking away from her. His smile was replaced with a look of indifference.

Keturah sighed, turning back to Nissa. After stomping, a while longer, she moved to the edge of the vat. "I think we've done our job. I suppose it's time to finish and then get the dinner ready."

Nissa looked at Joash and then back at her. Her expression was solemn, as she helped Keturah out of the vat.

When Keturah noticed the stains on the bottom of her feet, she smiled again and picked up her sandals. Lifting her skirts, she began to run barefoot toward the river. "Let's wash them at the creek." She looked over, as Joash watched her run past. The expression on his face was unreadable.

Nissa grabbed her sandals and laughed, chasing after Keturah over the meadow to the water's edge.

Both young women flew across the field and down into the water, letting out squeals when their feet hit the water.

Keturah sat by the bank, rubbing her feet in the cool creek, as Nissa took a place beside her.

She looked up onto the hill where Joash was working. "He almost seemed happy a moment ago. I'd not seen him smile like that before." She rubbed her foot some more.

Nissa beamed. She tapped Keturah with her finger.

"No." Keturah shook her head. "Not because of me."

Nissa smiled again. She pointed to her heart and then to Joash.

"Just the opposite. He seems to wish he never brought me here."

She dipped her feet back into the water and swished them around, then looked back up the hill at Joash working. "He's so untrusting and angry. But, seems to hide a lot of what he feels."

Nissa nodded, looking solemn.

Keturah let out a breath, as she swished her feet one more time in the water. "If he'd turn to the Lord. He'd be different."

Nissa eyes began to shine. She took Keturah's hand and squeezed it.

"Well, maybe someday. But, I suppose that'll take some time." She strapped on her sandals and stood, waiting for Nissa to follow. "Come. Your mother will need help with the meal."

Both young women made their way back to the house under Joash's watchful eye. Keturah breathed a silent prayer as she walked past, asking the Lord to change his heart.

***

Keturah scooted closer to the dinner table, and then looked up at the door, wondering where Joash was.

Mary and Simeon and Nissa had already begun to eat after the blessing.

Mary looked at the door and then at Keturah. "He's finishing a few things."

Keturah lifted the spoon of meaty stew to her lips and blew on it.

As she did, the door opened, and Joash came in the room. He leaned a couple working tools against the door, closed it behind him and then made his way around the table. He dropped down onto the mat next to her.

Keturah coughed at the cloud of dust and the smell of animals he brought in with him. She put the spoon back on the table and narrowed her eyes.

He looked at Keturah. "What?"

And then he laughed and took a wedge of bread from a basket on the table, shoving it into his mouth and chewing on it.

Keturah didn't say anything, but instead lifted her braid over her shoulder to the opposite side of him and ignored his question.

He reached over and touched her cheek with his hand.

Keturah drew back and pushed his arm away, rubbing her face.

Joash began to grin as he hungrily eyed the rest of the food on the table.

His mother gave him an annoyed look and waved a large, wooden spoon she picked up from the table, at him. "Keep your hands off her and the food. You're dirty and smell like that horse." The brow of her eye curved upward. "And I'm sure Keturah doesn't appreciate eating half the field with her meal."

Keturah mouthed another quick prayer to keep from beating him with her own spoon and got up. "I'll eat another time. I don't feel hungry now."

"You *were* eating. Sit back down."

She backed away from the table, and edged her way to the door, all the while eying the food on his plate. "No. Have your meal, first. I'll wait."

Joash gave her a stony stare.

Mary looked at Joash. "Go, and come back when you're clean." She waved the spoon at him again. "So, she can eat in peace."

He let out a snort. "Why should I suffer because of her?" He reached out to take a piece of goat cheese on a platter in the middle of the table, but his mother cracked him on the hand with the spoon.

He pulled back his hand. "Ow!" His frown was replaced with a look of astonishment.

Then, he eyed his mother's stern expression, as she gripped the utensil tightly in her hand, and he began to laugh.

He gestured for Keturah to sit back down. "Fine. I'll bathe and then tend to my stomach. You eat first."

Keturah lowered her eyes, her lashes fluttering against her cheeks. "But, I didn't mean…"

But, before she could finish her sentence, he rolled his eyes and laughed again. "Stop. Just sit and eat. I know when I'm beat. There are too many women in this place to win." He got up and brushed past her, taking a quick path to the door.

After he went out, Keturah sat back down. Mary and Nissa and she exchanged knowing glances, smiling.

Simeon chuckled as he eyed them, and then looked at the door. "I suppose he'll learn in time. It takes longer with some."

The women didn't say anything, but continued to smile as they ate.

Keturah breathed another prayer of thanks. The Lord would care for her.

*****

"Now faith is the substance of things hoped for, the evidence of things not seen." Hebrews 11:1 King James's Version

Chapter 20

That evening, Keturah went to the altar. As the sun lowered in the sky, she poured her heart out to the Lord and asked for his guidance and protection. Despite any hardships she endured after having been away from her home and family, she felt close to Adonai and knew he was watching over her. There was a chill in the air, and she tugged her wrap tighter around her, kneeling in front of the tall altar.

When she heard a voice behind her, she lifted her head and turned, surprised.

"You're here again?"

Joash moved next to her looking up at the large stone. A wry smile formed on his face, and his eyes glinted green. "For what?"

She didn't answer at first. She smoothed out her dress, eying him solemnly. "To be with the Lord."

He took a piece of grass and chewed on it lazily, eying her with skepticism. "But, you can't even see him. Don't you think it's foolish to believe in something not there?"

"Our forefathers hoped for things not seen. How could you doubt?" She felt the conviction of her words and prayed silently for the Lord to give her wisdom.

He laughed. "There are a lot of good reasons not to believe."

She sighed. Joash certainly didn't seem to be looking for answers, and she wasn't prepared to give them. She looked out into the fields. How anyone could deny the Lord, knowing the beauty of the creation? When her eyes rested on the creek in the distance, she realized the Lord's imprint was on many things.

And then, in the rippling stream, she suddenly knew the Lord had given her an answer.

She pointed. "Look." She didn't take her eyes from the creek. "See how it moves with no wind?"

He followed her gaze and stared back at her. "A force in nature." He eyed her curiously.

She nodded. "Yes. But, can you tell me what it looks like? The force?"

"I think you already know the answer to that."

She pushed back the dark curls that fell over her shoulder. Her voice was quiet. "I can't see the Lord either, but I know he's there. I feel his presence, like the force." She let out a contented sigh, thinking of the closeness she felt with Adonai, especially when she prayed. "If a person can believe in the force, they can believe in the Lord."

The lines tightened around Joash's mouth, and he turned to her. "If he's truly real, then why doesn't he care for you, and take you out of situations you don't want to be in? How does anyone hope in that kind of God?"

Keturah lifted her chin at an angle. "How do I know why he gives us the place in life he does? Maybe to make me stronger in trials, or to send me here because you needed me, is why. I don't know."

She turned to stare at him. "Who am I to question the Lord Almighty?"

She got up and went to him. "We'll all die sometime. Does it really matter what happens when we're here?" She stared at him with a confidence she knew was not her own.

He had an odd mixture of uncertainty and regard for her in his expression, and it was as if he didn't quite seem to know how to respond.

He reached down, taking a strand of her hair in his hand and pulled her closer to him. "You believe in the Lord, if that's what you want. But, don't try and get me to."

And then he whispered in her ear. "I only want what I can see and touch, what's real to me. It's what I can believe in." He leaned down and kissed the nape of her neck, trailing his hand down her back and pulling her closer and then lifted her into his arms. He followed the path in the direction of their home, taking her with him, as the sun began to slip downward, sending deep crimsons and violets over the horizon.

It bothered Keturah that she felt herself weakening in the physical sense to him, like a betrayal of her own self. And yet, when she breathed in the scent of lilies of the fields and felt the warmth of him next to her, she curled up in his arms. Despite Joash's openly gruff behavior toward those around him, he seemed to have a hidden, tender side that presented itself to her on occasion. And one of those times was when they were alone together. She sighed at the frailty in her own disposition when he was near.

*****

"And do not be drunk with wine, in which is dissipation; but be filled with the Spirit." Ephesians 5:18 King James's Version

Chapter 21

Keturah woke early the next morning to work outside in the courtyard. Joash came out the door, and headed past her toward the gate. She was carrying a metal pot filled with water into the house. She set it down on the ground. "Can you take it?"

Joash eyed her impatiently.

Keturah looked at the iron pot, knowing he'd have no problem carrying it inside. "I only need it past the door."

He let out an annoyed sound and brushed past her.

Even though she wanted to dump the water from it onto his head, she bit back a retort. She lifted it back up and began to half drag it past him. After a couple steps, she set it back on the ground and waited. She refused to look at him, as she stared at the arched doorway of the house and then leaned down to lift it again.

He let out an agitated breath and went to her, reaching to take the handle.

But, before he could, she pulled it away. "No." She began dragging it as far as she could and setting it back down. "You didn't want to. I can do it."

Joash's lip curled upward and he sneered, this time shoving her gently out of the way and lifting the pot and taking it into the house.

Keturah followed him in.

After he set it down, he moved past her and made his way toward the arched opening of the door to go back outside. But before he did, he turned back. "Next time, don't fill it so full." He said it in a low voice. "And don't ask for anything else."

Keturah bit her lip. She refused to treat him the way he treated her and stoop to his level. She said a quick prayer to the Lord, to keep from going after him and throttling him within an inch of his life.

Instead, she knelt down and let out a quiet breath. "Thank you." She looked up at him appreciatively, pushing her hair behind her.

He gave her a perturbed look, not saying anything, then turned and left through the door.

She let out a breath and went back to her work. "Thank you, Lord for curbing my tongue, which I've no power over and showing him your goodness and grace."

**

Joash stormed out of the courtyard and went to the stable, kicking the bench inside. He pulled on the collar of his robe, as if it were tight about his neck and bristled at the thought of being cooped up in the house for one more meal.

Keturah had to have known what she was doing. He wanted none of her sweet gestures and repentant looks.

When would he get called to his post, again? It seemed like ages since he'd been away from this place.

He looked at his horse and went over to her, reaching out and patting the side of her head.

Maybe a trip into town would suffice? It might do him good to see his friends.

He led his animal out after readying it for the ride and pulled himself onto its broad back.

The horse whinnied and pranced, excited to be going out, stomping at the ground beneath her.

He looked back toward the house once, and then set out on the path in the opposite direction. Maybe he'd find solace in a bit of drink and carousing, far from this place that seemed to have a stranglehold on him lately.

**

Keturah lifted her head from the straw mattress beneath her. She thought she heard the snort of a horse. It had to be the middle of the night, as dark as it was. There was definitely the sound of hooves clopping against the clay path. She went out the door to see if Joash had returned.

In the darkness, she eyed the shadowy figure of her husband sitting atop his horse. She was surprised to see he was ambling from side to side and slurring his words, mumbling to himself.

She put her hand over her mouth, and her eyes widened as he got off the animal and staggered toward the stable. He was drunk, and he swore under his breath as he kicked the gate open, making an angry sound.

She shuddered. It was bad enough he treated her unfairly when he was sober. What would he do lost to the strong wine's effects?

A New Dance

She crept into the darkness and found her way across the courtyard. She quietly hid behind a tree. When Joash came out and stumbled into the house, she edged her way into the stable, closing the gated door behind her and went to the back of it. It smelled strongly of animal and was dark and cold, yet there was comfort here. It would most likely offer her more protection than her own pallet this night.

She curled up in a corner pen on a bed of straw and pulled her wrap tighter around her. She shivered in the cool air, and lay awake for hours until she could no longer keep her eyes open. Soon, she let herself drift into a restless sleep, holding her wrap tightly to her.

***

Joash woke to a pounding headache and groaned as he turned over on his pallet. He reached for Keturah, hoping she might brew him something warm to lessen the pain. He thought it odd that she wasn't with him. Why had she risen so early?

And then a thought occurred to him as he sat up bolt right. He hadn't remembered her in the room when he dropped onto the straw mattress the night before. He questioned her absence, and yet, in the state he was in, had done nothing to look for her. He recalled giving himself over to a deep slumber instead.

He shook the hair from his eyes and stood up, dressing quickly and headed for his parent's room and sister's pallet. He looked in, realizing Keturah wasn't with them.

He tried to recall if he saw her at all after he returned, but couldn't for the life of him remember anything. Something turned in the pit of his stomach, and he felt sick inside as he searched the home, finding no evidence of her. Where could she have gone?

He hoped in his state the night before, he hadn't done anything to her without knowing. He went out into the courtyard, and panic set in when he didn't see her there either.

He called out her name a couple times, until he noticed the gated door of the stable. He took long strides to the entrance and went inside. He searched the area and then found her, sound asleep on a pile of straw in the corner of the room. She was clutching the thin wrap she held in her hands around her, as if she were cold.

"Keturah?"

Joash went to her and took her in his arms, holding her close. "What are you doing?" He groaned.

She looked up, and her first reaction was to recoil from him, her eyes widening.

And then, relief stole over her, and she wrapped her arms around his waist tightly, letting out a sound.

He didn't say anything, but lifted her up. He felt how chilled she was, and it bothered him that he was most likely the cause of it. He needed to get her back to the house.

He took her inside and gently laid her down, covering her with a woolen blanket, then went to his sister, nudging her shoulder.

"Nissa." He tapped her again, his voice a whisper.

His sister turned over and stared at him oddly.

"It's Keturah." He pointed to the door. "She needs you."

Nissa quickly got up and grabbed an outer wrap, pulling it around her and left the room.

***

Mary eyed her son warily. "What was she doing in the stable?" Her eyebrow rose slightly.

Joash shrugged. "How do I know? I came home late is all, and don't remember it. Will she be all right?"

His mother sighed and nodded. "She will, no thanks to you." She got up and took the empty bowl from him, putting it on a tray to take to the river.

Joash eyed the door. "I'll be leaving, anyway. They want me to fight." He took his sling and sword from the corner of the room and started to the door.

Mary went to him. "You'll tell her you're leaving?"

He grunted. "I'll be late if I do. I need to be going. You tell her, mother." He felt a tinge of guilt, but reached for the latch to go out.

"You wronged her, and cannot even go to her and admit it."

"Mother, I have to leave. There isn't time." His voice softened. "Please. Talk to her for me."

"Joash? His mother called after him.

"What?"

"Be careful."

He turned and gave her a rueful smile. "I'll be fine. Don't worry."

He strode out the door and into the sunlight, looking back only once. He shook his head and let out a breath, as he led his horse out of the stable and got onto the back of it. What a coward he was, he thought. What was it that he feared?

*****

"A wife of noble character who can find. She is worth far more than rubies." Proverbs 31:10 King James's Version

Chapter 22

Joash ducked under the doorframe of Daniel's home. There was a warm fire crackling in the hearth, and Ruth sat at a hand mill, working quietly. One small window above sent a shaft of light into the room from outside. It was going to be evening soon. It took a moment for his eyes to adjust to the dimly lit room.

He went to his friend, shaking his hand. "It's been a time since we've seen each other. Will you be ready to leave in the morning?"

Daniel looked over at Ruth and nodded.

She put down what she was working on and went to them. "If you take a seat on the mats, I'll bring you the meal I prepared."

Daniel's eyes softened. "She chose to stay with me."

She began setting platters of barley bread, lentil stew and apricots, pressed and dried into cakes in front of them, as they sat at the low, wooden table. Daniel prayed before they ate, then handed Joash food to put on his plate.

Joash couldn't help noticing the looks exchanged between Daniel and Ruth as he chomped on the aromatic, spiced food and washed it down with wine. Neither could take their eyes from each other. His brow rose as he watched them.

"How long do you think we'll be gone this time?" Joash licked the syrup from the apricots off his finger.

Daniel reached for a piece of bread. "Hopefully, not too long."

Joash shook his head. "I suppose we'll need to wait and see."

When Ruth leaned over a watering jar from the floor, Daniel got up and crossed to where she was. "I'll get it."

She lifted it up. "No. It's all right. You sit down."

She went out through the doorway, as Daniel watched. He went back to the table and took a seat, keeping his eye on the door.

Joash's eyes narrowed. It bothered him that his friend seemed so affected by his wife that he'd leave him sitting there, eating alone. Daniel had always been a good sort, but he didn't consider what marriage would do to him.

A New Dance

He grunted, while chewing on a spoonful of stew. Then, he grinned. "You're playing the fool. Is she worth it?"

The tone of Daniel's voice lowered. "Don't speak wrongly of my wife. We're friends, but you won't be welcome here, unless you treat her right." He began chewing on the bread.

Joash curbed the look in his eye. Then he laughed, replying, "But we took them from Shiloh." He wiped food from his face with the back of his hand.

Daniel's expression said it all. His brow furrowed deeply, and he scowled. "Please. I know I did wrong then, but I treat her the way the Lord would want, now. And I expect my friends to do the same."

Joash looked puzzled and swallowed a piece of bread. He felt a surge of guilt run through him, but shrugged. "I'll do this for your sake. But, it won't happen with the one I have."

He took a drink of wine, enjoying the heady scent of it, lengthening his gulp.

Daniel sighed, looking at the door. "You do things as you see fit, but you'll reap what you sow. You shouldn't treat your wife wrongly, but give her the love she deserves."

Joash spooned out some more stew into his bowl and looked up. "Who says I love her?" He scooped a spoon of lentils into his mouth and began chewing. "Keturah doesn't care for me. She has what she needs."

"But, if you were kind, she might care for you."

Joash gave him a look of ire, but something stuck his throat when he went to reply. He thought of Keturah's expression and the tears on her face the last time he talked to her. He took another bite and then gulped down more wine.

He turned, when the door swung open.

Ruth came back in the room, and she immediately sought out Daniel. She placed the jar near them, and her eyes lit as she looked at him.

Daniel got up from the table. "Mother will take care of the food. I want to see you before I leave." He took her by the arm and then turned to Joash. "I'll be out with the horses at daylight. There's a pallet for you on the roof to sleep on." He pointed to a wooden ladder, leading up to the top of the house. "We'll talk again in the morning."

Joash nodded.

"We're glad you came." Daniel smiled, and then left with Ruth to an inner room.

Joash pushed the hair out of his eyes and found his way up the ladder to the pallet on the top of the roof. He lay on his back, looking up at the stars. It felt good to get out of that dark room, out in the fresh air. One more knowing glance between Daniel and Ruth would have made him sick, and he was relieved the evening had drawn to a close.

What did his friend know? Someday, Daniel might find Ruth not so faithful. And where would that leave him?

He let out a breath and rolled his eyes.

He pulled the fur blanket at the end of the pallet over him and groaned. Not only did he have to watch them staring at each other all evening, now he had to endure the night alone. He let out a sound and growled to himself, annoyed by his conflicting feelings.

He looked at the horizon and into the night sky. A cloud was passing over the lower part of the moon, making it a sliver. Most of the sky was bright, and the stars were covering the expanse of it. Crickets were chirping, and there was an occasional hoot of a lonely owl in the distance.

He frowned, when he thought of Keturah. Despite what he told Daniel, he knew he should be treating her better. She didn't deserve what she got. She never asked to be his wife, and she took the role almost willingly. But, he didn't plan on changing. And she shouldn't expect it.

He wondered if she were asleep, and looked back up at the stars. And then he let out a low sound. He didn't like the fact that there was an empty feeling inside him tonight. Some of the times he was with Keturah he began to feel something in him stir for her, and that bothered him. And now tonight, he almost wished she were near.

The acrid smell of smoke drifted past him from the hole in the roof. No scent of flower petals next to him, or fragrance of spices from the meal she cooked; just charred wood and burning embers.

He'd better watch it, he groaned. He'd be acting like Daniel. He needed to push thoughts of her out of his head, or his nights away from her these months would seem even lonelier.

"And this is one of the reasons why I didn't want a wife."

***

A New Dance

Joash laid his spear and sling next to him, as he sat on the side of a cliff, listening to the other soldiers below. They howled with laughter around the crackling campfires further down the mountain. For some reason, he didn't feel like celebrating tonight.

It was dark from where he sat, and the only light was from the full moon and stars that peppered the sky. He sought out the city of Bethel in the distance. He could see a dim glow and a few lamps that were still lit. It was quiet up on the hill where he was.

"Joash!" one of the men slurred. "Come! Drink with us!"

He didn't answer, but listened to them making crude jokes. He shook his head, annoyed. He was better off away from them.

His muscles ached after the skirmish today, and he tended to his arm that had taken a wound. It was sore, but would heal. It'd be better by the time he was home again.

He let out a breath, his jawline tightening. He turned over, staring into the night. He tried to push out thoughts of Keturah, but couldn't.

Daniel's words haunted him like a battering pole. You'll reap what you sow, he'd said. You shouldn't treat her like that.

The words sunk deep, when he remembered how many nights he'd heard Keturah weep quietly before she went to sleep. And he hadn't forgotten the look in her eyes when he'd brought her from the stable. She surely didn't look at him the way Daniel's wife did.

He'd noticed her giggling with Nissa and laughing with her father the other day. But, with him it was different. He didn't doubt that if she had the chance, she'd leave him and go back to Shiloh in an instant, if he let her.

But, it was better to not allow his feelings into it. He knew the consequences of love and loss. It made more sense to leave those things alone.

And yet, sometimes when he watched Daniel and realized how content he was, Joash wondered if such a thing was possible for him.

He stood up, pacing on the rock ledge. He was tired of thinking about it.

He picked up his weapons and started down to the campfires.

The men were quieting and taking to their pallets. There'd be things to do, tomorrow. It was time to get back to his tent and sleep.

*****

99

"Be not as the horse, or as the mule, which have no understanding: whose mouth must be held with bit and bridle, lest they come near unto thee." Psalm 32:9 King James's Version

Chapter 23

After months away, Joash was apprehensive about returning home and seeing Keturah. He couldn't get the image of her the night before he left, out of his mind. It bothered him that she'd chosen to sleep in the dark, cold stable instead of with him. But, he couldn't very well blame her for steering clear of him that night.

The more time he spent with her, it was difficult to deny her beauty both on the outside and the inside. She showed faithfulness to him, even when he deserved none of it, when he could clearly see that she wasn't happy with the things he did.

The past was like a weight he carried around on his shoulders, and he wrestled with the thought of it. He'd told himself he wouldn't allow the same things to happen again, and yet, with Keturah he found his defenses lowering. Something about her, made him want to be different and to treat her differently than he had.

He'd liked to think he was happy before he met her, not answering to anyone, and living as he wished. Yet, after the visit to Daniel's home and watching the empty shells of drunken men he spent time with outside of Bethel, he couldn't help feeling as if there was something missing in his life. For both the sake of his own self-preservation and that of his wife and family, he decided changes were in order.

***

With Joash gone, Keturah was free to do as she pleased while he was away. She actually enjoyed herself in his absence.

She spun around in her new linen tunic, a beautiful blue color with embroidered flowers on the sleeves and around the hem. She was in one of the smaller rooms of the house. She grabbed a yellow tie to wrap around her waist and then put on the gold necklace her father had given her. She fingered it reverently, wondering what he and the others in her family were doing at this time.

A New Dance

She motioned to her sister. When Nissa came to her, she hugged her and smiled. "Thank you. It's beautiful. I want your mother to know how much I love it, too."

Nissa nodded and squeezed her hand, her brown eyes dancing.

"And my hair. I've never worn it this way." Nissa had pulled back two small braids and attached them with a beautiful, wooden clasp. She let the rest flow long over her shoulders and placed tiny yellow flowers in the braided sections.

Joash's mother came into the room. Her face lit up, and she let out a sound. "How beautiful you look, Keturah." And then she sighed. "I wish my son treated you better. He spends too much time warring and destroying things, and now I fear he won't ever know how to care for a woman."

Keturah went to her and took her hand. "Don't worry, mother. Maybe someday he'll understand." She said the words, but didn't believe them. It'd take a miracle for that hardheaded man to change. She was glad he'd been out of town, but dreaded the fact that he'd be home this evening, in time for one of the festivals. She'd planned to spend the day with Nissa, but now would probably be forced to spend it with him.

When she finished, she grabbed the tunic she was working on and a spindle of the thread she'd made from goat hair. "Come, Nissa. Let's go to the courtyard to embroider these. The sun will feel good. It's a beautiful day outside."

Nissa grabbed the needles made from bone and partially sewn garments and headed out to the courtyard behind Keturah.

They sat down on a stone step and began to work. There wasn't a cloud in the sky. Chickens were clucking and pecking the grain spread out for them on ground just outside the courtyard, and two of the goats trotted freely around them within a walled area next to the house.

Keturah watched Joash's sister work quietly. She wondered at her muteness. She felt bad how Joash treated her. She couldn't blame Nissa for not wanting to say anything to him.

"I wish you could talk." Keturah put down the cloth she was working on. "I'd love to know what you think of your brother."

Nissa smiled. She pointed to a donkey in the small gate at the end of the courtyard where the goats were.

Keturah's eyes widened. "Like the donkey? Joash?"

Nissa nodded and pointed to her mouth and then at the animal.

"Well, he does bray like one." Keturah sighed.

Nissa began to laugh. She nodded again, her eyes sparkling. She tightened her fists, showing her muscles, tipping from side to side.

Keturah giggled. "Exactly, like a mule! All brawn, and what he says is ridiculous."

Nissa let out another laugh, and Keturah joined in. Both were giggling, so hard they could barely stop, when they noticed Joash had come in from outside the gate and was watching them. He stood there for a moment, as if not sure what to make of them.

He called to her. "Keturah!"

She went to him with a wary look in her eye and stopped a few paces from him.

"Closer. I want to greet my wife."

She eyed his dusty, work-worn clothing and the sweat seeping through his tunic and backed up a step. "Not until you clean up."

He looked bothered at first, and then his eyes swept over her new clothes and hair appraisingly, and he patted his horse. "I suppose I should care for Betsalel, first. She seems to need me more than you do."

"Betsalel? The name of your horse?" She looked perturbed.

He eyed her both puzzled and amused. He stroked the horse's neck. "She's dark like a shadow."

"But, you can't have that name."

"What? I've always called her that." He tossed his head back and laughed. "I can't change my horse's name."

"But, it's my goat's name. And it's a boy's name. You can't have it." Her cheeks turned crimson, and her eyes were dark. Joash took her from her home and her parents and all she held dear, and now he'd stolen the name of her pet. She felt as if everything she had, he found a way to take and destroy. But, he couldn't take Betsalel's name, too. A tear dropped down on her cheek. "You can't have it." And then her voice dropped to a whisper. "Because it's mine."

He reached out to wipe the tear away.

But, before he could touch her, she thrust out her arm, holding the bone needle clenched in her hand, ready to strike him.

Her dark eyes were hard, and she bit out the words. "I said *not* to touch me." She glowered at him.

Joash took a quick step toward her and caught her wrist with his hand and squeezed it until she dropped the needle. He pulled her close and eyed her dangerously. "Don't ever do that again."

Nissa ran off to the house, crying.

His grip loosened, but he still held her there.

She could smell the grit and trail of dust coming from him. He'd stolen so much from her and demanded so much. How could she ever live with him for years to come?

Keturah lowered her head. Her eyes were fixed on the ground and she began to weep, trying to wipe her tears with her free hand. "It's only that you have taken everything."

There was a moment where he didn't say anything. He lowered her arm, and it seemed as if he would try and comfort her by reaching out to her with his other hand, and then decided against it.

He let her go of her instead and took the horse's reigns and stalked off.

Keturah crumpled to the ground in tears.

***

Joash pounded the side of the wall of the stable and then sat down on the bench inside. His horse's name, had sparked an argument?

He reached out and brushed the side of his animal's fur coat. He looked at the horse and shook his head. "I came back to make changes. But with her, how is this possible?"

He lifted his hands to his head and held them there.

She needed to let go of her precious Shiloh. Women were taken from their villages all the time. She knew this. She knew the Benjamite's plight. And as long as she had a home and family to go to, it should've been enough.

True, he'd not treated her like Daniel treated Ruth, but he'd come home with the intentions of making amends, and she'd not even given him a chance.

And what was it with Nissa? When he'd walked through the gate, his sister, who hardly ever acknowledged him, was laughing and joking over something Keturah had said. Now, the two of them appeared to be best of friends.

He stared at the rock walls of the stable. He got up and pulled the reigns from the horse's neck and wound them around his hand. He set them on a shelf built into the wall.

He took the covering off his head and pushed his hand through his hair.

Keturah was a beautiful woman, with her dark hair and eyes and rosy cheeks. When she came to the gate, it was difficult for him to hold back from her. He'd expected things to be different, but he'd not even been given the chance.

He should have backed away when she held up the needle. But, right away he'd lost his temper. He let out a sigh exasperated, and then a light laugh. Why couldn't he have left that alone? Did he always have to win?

He shrugged. Too many years of fighting, and he couldn't back down. He sprung too quickly and was too used to being in command of others.

He didn't understand how to deal with Keturah, and he wasn't sure he wanted to.

He stood up, shaking his head.

Tonight, there was the festival. For the first time in a long time, he thought it might be good to offer some type of prayer to the Lord. Nothing in life prepared him for any of this.

*****

"For thou wilt save the afflicted people; but wilt bring down high looks." Psalm 18:27 King James Version

Chapter 24

When Joash greeted Keturah later that evening, he was in a new, striped tunic, one she'd never seen. He'd rid himself of the sweat and dust from the trail, and his ordinarily mussed hair was combed into place.

Regardless of his coarse behavior and the way his cool, green eyes assessed her so thoroughly whenever she was near, she couldn't help the sight of him making her take a breath and step back. If he were ever to change his ways and become like his father and treat her kindly, she knew she'd be at his mercy for the rest of her life.

He strode over to her and put out his arm. "Come. I'll take you around Bethel to the festival. To show you off to friends."

She sighed, taking his arm. Did he realize that the things he said to her, were never what she wanted to hear?

He pulled her into the courtyard with him, and they waited for Nissa and his parents to join them.

Keturah stared at the stars, which looked like speckled patterns across the sky. The night air had a sweet, damp smell and was cool, enough to make her shiver.

Joash's eyes swept over her, but not in the way she was used to. "Wait. I'll be back."

She didn't answer him.

He left to go back in the home, disappearing through the doorway, leaving her standing alone in the darkness to wait for him.

It was quiet in the courtyard, save for a few animals calling out from their pens next to the house and the rustle of the bushes in the light wind. The moon was luminous and almost round. It sent beams downward and lit most of the area where she stood, other than the shadowy corners.

She moved her sandaled foot against the ground in a slow, fluid movement, enjoying the rhythm of the night sounds. Her heart beat softly in her chest, while she felt music inside her, and she wished she could dance.

But, she stopped. There were footsteps again.

"Mother and father and Nissa will be here in a moment. We'll walk with them."

She nodded looking down at Joash's hands and gave him an odd look.

He was holding a brown woolen shawl and went to her, placing it clumsily around her shoulders. He seemed somewhat uncomfortable and shrugged. "You'll be warmer with this."

Keturah nodded, wondering what he was up to. She took the cloth in her hands and pulled it around her, eying him quizzically. "You didn't have to get it for me."

He shrugged, and a lazy smile spread over his face.

Keturah wondered what he was thinking.

They both turned when Nissa ran out of the doorway to them. She stood at Keturah's side, waiting for her parents.

Not long after, Simeon and Mary came into the courtyard.

"Should we go, now?" Mary asked to no one in particular.

They all nodded.

The family set out on the path together, as they headed to the festival down the street.

Keturah eyed the scarf around her shoulders. She looked up at Joash again, still not sure what to think. He took her hand and pulled her to him as they walked.

The path to the temple courtyard was lit with large lamps. There was music and feasting, and the people there were sharing stories and the latest news with each other. Keturah thought of her home and family. Her eyes moistened with tears, and she wiped at them.

Joash stared at her and lifted her chin. His hand curved around her neck, and his fingers smoothed back her hair. "What's wrong?"

She opened her eyes obediently and met his with her own. Sounds of the festival permeated the air around them, and she couldn't help remembering the last time she'd heard the same music, dancing in the vineyards.

He looked annoyed. "It's feast day. A time to enjoy yourself."

She tried to turn away, but he held her there.

"I miss my family, my father, mother and two brothers. And I miss my little pet, Betsalel. We went to festivals together."

He stroked her hair, and she thought there was something tender in his eyes, but then it disappeared. He let out a sound.

"Remember. We're your family, now. You need to let go of your past. Shiloh's not your home anymore."

She took her hand from his arm and tensed. Did he have any feelings at all? "Shiloh will always be my home. And you'll never be my family."

She started to walk away. Then in the crowd of people, there was a familiar laugh.

Tirzah? She'd know that sound anywhere. She looked around. Where was she?

Joash caught her arm, but she pulled away. "No! Let go!"

She turned away. Her scarf slid down her shoulder, and she lifted it around her.

He gripped her hand tightly and pulled her to his side. "Don't walk away from me, Keturah."

She lifted her foot and stomped hard on the top of his sandals.

He let go of her. "Ow!" He went after her, trying to grab the back of her tunic, but missed and latched on to her hair instead.

"Keturah?" Tirzah jumped up from the mat where she was sitting and pushed Joash, who let go. "Get away from her!"

Joash's mother stepped in. "What are you are doing, Joash?"

He took a step back. "Trying to stop her from leaving." He had an exasperated expression on his face.

When Keturah saw her friend, she flew into Tirzah's arms, ignoring Joash's explanations. "Oh! You don't know how glad I am to see you." She started weeping.

Tirzah patted her back and smoothed out her hair. "There, there friend. Things will be all right now. You'll see."

When Keturah finally quit crying, Tirzah held Keturah back from her, and she pushed the tears from her face. "It's not so bad, is it?"

Keturah looked up at Joash ruefully.

Tirzah went over to him. "What've you done?" She stood there with her fists clenched and ready to strike.

Joash stared at Tirzah without answering.

His father stepped in. "Joash. It seems you find a fight, even when there is none."

Joash let out a breath and stared off in the distance.

Well, this was new, Keturah thought.

He looked as if he was going to try and redeem himself, but closed his mouth instead. When his eyes lifted to Keturah's, they almost seemed be pleading with her for help.

He hadn't actually done anything at the festival. For one of the few times, she felt a measure of sympathy for him.

She spoke quietly to Tirzah. "I heard your laugh. He didn't know I was trying to find you."

And then she turned to Simeon. "It was a misunderstanding."

Mary shook her head. "Well, this is good. I thought Joash was in trouble again."

Simeon smiled. "Yes, well, let's take a seat."

They turned to join the crowd at the mats.

Keturah took Joash's arm and spoke quietly to Tirzah. "This is my husband."

Joash eyed Keturah as if pleased. He pulled her close. "We met in Shiloh."

Keturah's eyes darkened. *Met* in Shiloh? She just saved him from Tirzah, and now she wanted to rein blows upon him.

"Well, maybe *met* wasn't the right word." He looked down at her, a sardonic grin widening on his face, as he tightened his hold on her.

Keturah gave him an annoyed look, but couldn't pull away.

Tirzah just stood there staring at him and then at Keturah for a long moment, and then she let out a loud giggle and then began laughing hysterically.

"Tirzah?"

Tirzah held her stomach, as a tall, dark-haired man took a place by her side.

"And now, what have you found to amuse yourself with. I'm Tirzah's husband, Isaac."

Tirzah stopped laughing and looked up. "Oh, it is nothing." She had a mischievous look on her face.

"What is so funny?" Keturah practically shouted at her.

Tirzah held back another laugh. And then, eyed Joash curiously. "When I said you needed someone different than Hiram, this isn't exactly what I meant." She put her hand over her mouth and giggled.

Joash's eyes narrowed. His voice was a low growl. "Hiram?" His hand clenched, and the muscles in his arm tightened.

Keturah put her hand to the side of his face. "Tirzah didn't even like him."

Tirzah's eyes danced. "Oh, he wasn't so bad." And then she laughed. "But, this one? He is not anything like him."

Joash shook his head and let go. He grumbled to himself. "And for this, I've come home. I may as well have stayed away."

Keturah ignored his statement. She smiled at Tirzah, then ran and hugged her. "I'd know your laugh, anywhere. I'm so glad to see you again."

The man next to Tirzah put out his hand to Joash who shook it. "Tirzah isn't so mild mannered. You should count yourself lucky."

Tirzah turned to Isaac and took his arm in hers. "You deserve someone like me." Then, she turned to Joash. "Isaac and I *met* in Shiloh, too."

Keturah rolled her eyes. It was going to be a long night.

*****

"Thou hast ravished my heart, my sister, my spouse; thou hast ravished my heart..." Song of Solomon 4:9 King James Version

Chapter 25

The next day, after the mid-morning meal, Keturah and Nissa followed Joash to a field. He had handed each of them a bag of seeds that they'd slung from their shoulders.

The day was still relatively cool. Keturah and Nissa walked behind him scattering seeds in the shallow trenches he dug with his stone tool.

Keturah eyed him just ahead of them. He seemed so at ease with physical labor, by the way he moved, never stopping to take a breath. The muscles in his arms tightened as he pushed on the end of the stick and he dragged the stone at the end of it into the ground, his long legs easily making their way down the garden rows.

He caught her staring at him, a gleam entering his eyes and then turned and went back to work.

She threw more seeds on the path, bothered by her conflicted feelings. Mostly, she wanted to be as far from him as she could, but there were times she felt compelled to know more about him and understand what had caused him to be the way he was. Something kept telling her that he wasn't as hard-hearted as she first thought. He even seemed civil at the festival the night before.

And because of the time they spent lately, she was responding to him in ways that contradicted how she felt about him. She didn't seem to have control over it.

She tried to quell the sensation that ran through her, as she watched him, annoyed by her reaction. It didn't seem fair that he could have this type of affect on her, even when he didn't seem to care for her.

Nissa was watching her, so she went back to what she was doing. She hoped the girl hadn't read her thoughts.

As the sun moved higher into the sky, she began to feel warm. She drew a hand across her brow, looking out over the land. Beyond the garden, there were wildflowers of purples and whites moving in waves in the breeze. She thought of home. She wondered what her family was doing.

A New Dance

Then, Keturah looked down. There was a rock in the path. She reached out to Nissa. "Watch out!"

But, it was too late. Nissa stumbled on the jagged stone before Keturah could stop her. The girl let out a little sound, and the seeds from her sack spilled onto the ground beneath her, mixing into the dark soil.

Keturah stopped to help her up. "Are you all right?"

Nissa nodded.

Joash looked at the ground, eying the seeds lying scattered on the path. He threw down the tool in his hand and started toward them.

"What have you done?" He set his eyes on his sister. "Don't you know how important those are?"

Nissa started scrambling to pick the seeds up and put them into her shoulder bag. She turned a pale color, clearly distressed.

Joash scowled. "Answer me, Nissa!"

He reached down and took her arm. "Just speak! I know you can!" He towered above her.

She looked at him helplessly, trying to pull away, but couldn't.

Keturah's heart went out to the girl. Nissa was like a small lamb facing a wolf. Something boiled up inside her.

She reached out and yanked his arm. "Leave her be, you Philistine! She's not going to speak to you, the way you treat her!" She pushed his shoulder, so he lost his balance.

Joash caught himself, but reached out and then, pulled her down to the ground with him. At first, he was furious, his hand going to the back of her neck and his eyes heated as he looked at her.

Did she go too far? She wished she'd curbed her tongue. She'd done so well lately. But, Nissa couldn't stand up to him.

She tried to loosen herself from his grip, but was unable. She looked up at him, her eyes large. "Your sister..." And her hands went to his chest. "I didn't mean..."

She began to tremble. "I'm sorry, Joash." She lowered her eyes and looked back up at him.

And then he drew her closer. She noticed the anger in him began to dissipate, and he was staring at her strangely. There was a spark in his eye. "Philistine?"

He reached up to push back a piece of her hair that had fallen loose from her braid. Then he let out a laugh, short at first, and then longer.

Nissa moved away from them and began putting seeds into her bag.

Keturah's heart thumped inside her. It was difficult to think with him so near. She was breathless. She said in a whisper, "I didn't mean..."

He let her go, and she stood, brushing herself off.

He didn't take his eyes from her as he got up from off the ground and went to her, encircling his hand around her waist and lowering his head to hers.

Her eyes widened at the way he was looking at her, and she felt the breath go out of her, when his mouth came down on hers in a stirring kiss that afterward trailed passionately down her neck.

Her body reacted in tingles, and she turned to him, cheeks blaming with heat.

And then, he buried his face in her hair, his breath in her ear, whispering to her. "There's your Philistine." His eyes were glistening. "And I see you liked it."

When he let her go, she backed away, speechless.

He turned from her and walked back to the hoe that he laid on the ground and picked it up, going back to his work. Then, he laughed again.

Keturah simmering inside with embarrassment as she lifted her own seed bag back onto her shoulder. She didn't look at either Joash or Nissa, but at the ground instead and began working.

Why would he do such a thing, and in front of his sister? What was he thinking?

She shook her head, trying to understand the emotions pouring through her. She clenched the strap on the bag she carried, staring at his broad back, maddened by his insensitivity.

She reached into her bag and pulled out more seeds, spreading them down the rows. She needed to pull herself together and think about the work there was to be done, and not about him.

She moved closer to Nissa, her eyes still on the ground. She watched carefully for rocks on the path, not wishing for a repeat performance. She'd not give Joash a chance for such behavior again.

*****

"Out of the south cometh the whirlwind: and cold out of the north." Job 37:9 King James's Version

Chapter 26

Afternoon approached, and they were nearly finished. Keturah eyed the last row with anticipation in her heart.

But before they reached the end, Joash stopped working and looked at the sky. He looked concerned.

There were some blackening clouds in the distance. A hot breeze rustled the low-lying bushes and whipped up dust on the ground. The air was steamy and moist.

He turned to Keturah and Nissa. "Go inside, and tell mother and father to do the same and stay there."

"What is it?" Keturah's eyes widened. "Are you coming?"

"I have to care for the animals first. The winds are coming. Go!"

Keturah grabbed Nissa's hand and pulled her along, as they made their way to the house. She glanced back to see Joash putting the horses and donkeys in the stable, along with the goats.

The wind was picking up and the storm clouds were getting closer. She began to run, but as they neared the courtyard, she looked into the fields again. Joash was on his way down to the pasture. She had to squint to see his form in the clouds of dust flying past him.

His parents were working in front of the house. Simeon was lifting a leather hide to dry over a wall, and Mary was working on a piece of cloth.

"Joash said there's a storm."

They both moved closer to Keturah.

Mary looked concerned. "Where is he?"

Keturah took her hand. "With the animals."

Simeon eyed the darkening the sky. "We can't wait." He put his arm around his wife and led her into the house.

Mary kept turning to watch the horizon, clearly distressed.

Keturah looked out behind her, as they stepped in the door. She didn't see Joash anywhere.

She had mixed feelings, and cringed at the thought that she was almost hoping something would happen and she'd never see him again.

She'd seen Mary's face. Joash's mother would be devastated if he didn't return. How could she think such a thing?

But if a tree fell or a whirlwind came, and he died in it, then, she'd be a widow and would be free to go back to Shiloh. She could see her family again.

She lifted her hands to her face. She felt sick inside and said a quick prayer for him.

She took one last look out the door and then shut it.

"He'll be here." Simeon moved away from the door. "Don't worry. Come, let's get by the fireplace."

Nissa and Keturah nodded and quickly knelt by the stone hearth.

Simeon brought the oil lamps from a table to where the women were sitting and found a place next to Mary. He put them on the floor.

Keturah could hear the sounds of wind picking up and rain beating the side of the house.

She watched the wooden door, framed in solid stone. The storm's roar outside grew louder. Her body tensed.

The flame on the lamp next to her flickered, as wind whistled through small cracks in the outer wall.

She scrunched the woven mat in her hand, tightening her fist around its edge.

Nissa pointed to the door, her face pale.

Keturah tried to comfort her by taking her hand. "He'll come." But, she was beginning to wonder. The storm was so heavy upon them now.

Then the entry way suddenly flew open, and Joash ducked under the stone frame, pushing the heavy wooden door shut behind him. He shoved damp hair back from his face and turned around, sweeping the room with his eyes.

Keturah just stared at him. A fleeting feeling of despair swept over her, and her heart weakened at his presence.

When spotted her, he seemed relieved at first. And then his eyes narrowed, as he studied her expression, and his mouth lifted at the corner.

He took off his outer wrap and hung it on a hook on the wall and went to the fireplace to warm his hands.

Sounds of hail hit the roof, and a louder chugging wailing came from outside the home.

The room got dark as the night, save for the small flickering light from the lamps.

Keturah felt pressure in her ears. She turned and instinctively drew her hands to her face, while crashes of lightning and loud sounds of thunder passed over them.

Joash's brow rose as he watched her from above, while he turned in front of the heat to dry his clothes.

Keturah was sure it was a whirlwind from the sounds outside. She wondered if it would do damage.

She tried to steady her breath as she looked around the dark room. Shelves against the wall were shaking, the clay dishes on them clattering, a couple falling to the floor and breaking. A piece of the ceiling came loose, and rain dripped through. But, the structure of the building held together, sturdy against the tempest outside.

A short time passed with more of the howling winds, and finally the storm began to subside and pass.

Keturah sighed, the knots inside her loosening when the wind outside died.

When she realized it was over, she quickly got up and brushed the reeds from the floor off her tunic and straightened the upper portion. She could feel Joash's eyes on her, but didn't look at him and moved away from him.

Simeon and Mary went to the door, opening it and looking out.

"Some large trees in the valley are down." Simeon turned back to them. "But, other than that, there's little damage. I'll go on the roof to see." He started climbing a tall, wooden ladder that led to the top.

Joash made his way to the door. "I let the goats roam free and have to get them back. There wasn't enough room for all of them in the stable."

Keturah sighed. She looked toward the door. It struck her again that things wouldn't be changing here, and she'd not be going back to Shiloh.

Joash shot her a dark look, as if he knew her thoughts and then reached for the latch and went out.

Nissa went to Keturah, tugging on her arm and pointing to the opening where her brother went.

Keturah's brow rose. "Go with him?"

Nissa nodded.

"He'll be all right."

Nissa nudged her arm, pushing her to the door.

Keturah looked out. "Nissa. He doesn't need me."

Nissa was solemn, and she looked down. She pulled on the sleeve of Keturah's tunic, again and pointed to the door.

Keturah sighed, and then shook her head. "Fine. I'll see if he needs anything. But only for you."

***

Keturah shivered as she spotted the large trees further down the valley ripped up by the roots and lying on their sides. The wind must have been strong to do such damage.

The rain stopped, and the sun had peeked out from behind a cloud. Most of the storm had moved into the distance and formed large bubbles of orange and gray clouds that covered the sky.

Joash was already out in the pasture carrying a long walking stick and calling to the animals. The flock was moving toward him, responding to his low, soothing voice. A larger one, near him, lifted his head and wailed. Joash bent to pet its fleecy head. It let out a baying sound, and he smoothed back its fur.

How good he was with the animals. Keturah saw how they responded to him. Sometimes, it didn't seem quite fair, that he had such love for them, the way he ruffled their ears and spoke to them in such a quiet, gentle manner, when he didn't seem to know how to treat his own family or her. Why Nissa wanted her to go to him, she didn't know.

She found her way down the side of the rocky hill to try and help. When she got to him, she stopped, realizing he was watching her.

She reached out and touched the side of one of the sheep. His fur was slightly wet, but soft to the touch.

Joash eyed her curiously. "Why did you come?"

She looked down and then turned away. "Nissa wanted me to."

"Oh." He frowned and went back to his work.

Then, she noticed one of the smaller sheep, limping with blood on its side. She let out a sound and went to it.

She tried to coax the animal to her, but it was afraid.

Joash went quickly to it, checking its leg and the place where the blood was. "It's only a scrape. He'll be fine." He began tending to it.

Keturah patted a white, curly haired lamb next to her and looked out over the flock. "Are they all here?"

"Most of them. But, I'll need to go look for the others once the flock is back in through the gate."

"Oh. I suppose I can't be much help to you."

Joash gave her an interested look and grinned. "Later you can." His green eyes glinted. "I missed you on the trail."

Keturah's mouth opened slightly, and she gave him an embarrassed look, as she felt the heat come into her cheeks. She was going to say something back, but instead spun on her heel and started back up the hillside, digging her sandals into the wet earth.

"Keturah…I…"

She clenched her fists and kept walking. Did he understand how the things he said bothered her?

There were footsteps behind, and she felt a tug on her arm. "I didn't mean to hurt you. But, I did miss you." His voice was low.

She didn't look up at him, wondering what had come over him lately. She wasn't sure if she could trust him, or if she wanted to.

She pulled away from him. "I have to get back."

He let go of her arm, and she hastily made her way to the courtyard.

She went into the home and sat by the fireplace, and took some goat hair that had been gathered into loose ropes from a basket. She started twisting it with a spindle into threads, and then wrapping it around the spindle for later use. And then she lowered it into her lap.

Simeon, Nissa and Mary were all outside, and she was left alone.

She bent her head and said a silent prayer. She wished her mother were here.

"Help me, Lord, to understand and love him. Tell me what to do."

*****

"Trust in the Lord with all thine heart; and lean not unto thine own understanding." Proverbs 3:5 King James's Version

Chapter 27

The next morning Keturah awoke, and Joash wasn't there. She got up and went to the door, looking out. He was practicing with his stone and sling. She couldn't help being intrigued by the way he worked, never missing a chance to practice.

He put the stone in the sling and drew it back, his arm flexed as he held it there. And then he let it go; hitting the tree he was aiming at. He took three more shots, all striking the spot within the marked space.

There were times it was difficult not to feel admiration for him. Her expression was wistful. Since he'd come home, she noticed changes in him she was beginning to like. She couldn't really explain it, but there was something about him that was different. He was showing her more courtesy than he ever had.

He turned. Seeing her in the entrance, his expression changed, and he started toward the house.

Keturah waited there until he came in the door.

He put his bow and sling on the bench and went to her, drawing her near, his head bent to hers. "I meant to thank you for keeping your friend Tirzah at bay the other evening." There was a gleam in his eye.

Keturah eyed him solemnly. She wanted to respond in kind, but held back, still wary. The man she met in Shiloh was very different from this one. "Tirzah can be protective."

He gave her his usual amused expression. "Most people around you can be. Somehow, you've gained them all under your trust."

"I'm sure they feel sorry for me, because of you." Her eyes met his with a bit of a challenge.

He chuckled, taking her hand in his.

She didn't like the way he was looking at her. More like the old Joash.

Keturah let out a breath. She started to walk away. "I've chores to do. Your mother and I are washing clothes this morning, and we have a lot to do."

He reached out and stopped her. "It can wait."

Keturah moved toward the door again. "No. I should help."

Joash was there before she could leave, ignoring her protests. "Stay with me." He leaned down and brushed his lips against hers. "Please."

It bothered her how she responded to his touch, her cheeks warming to his smile, as if knowing the power he held over her. She didn't know how to answer, so said nothing, and stayed. She'd come to an aggravating realization that she really didn't want to go, but was reticent to admit it to him.

A spark lit his eye. "So you agree the chores can wait, and that there will be time for them later."

Her look was a mix of anticipation and frustration at the same time. "I'll stay."

Joash took a strand of her hair and pulled her close. "I'm glad."

***

The next day, Joash barely spoke, as he got ready to leave. He took a bow and a sling from the corner of the room and strode to the door.

Keturah woke and rubbed her eyes, sitting up. "Where are you going?"

Joash gripped his armor to him and turned. He looked back at her with a hard, cynical expression. "Out."

Keturah thought things had been better lately between them, and that he might begin to confide in her more. He left often and never told anyone where he was going, and it was difficult to know what to expect from him. She never knew when he was coming back. "But, what if we need to find you? I might want to know."

Joash seemed conflicted. He stared at her a moment and then took one of his weapons off the table. He didn't reply.

"Or need to know where you are." She thought she might have seen a glimmer of something in his eyes akin to guilt.

But, then he backed up and grabbed the door again. "I need to go."

Keturah lifted the wool covering around her tighter.

Joash opened the door and then looked back. "Keturah, I've never had to answer to anyone, and I'm not starting now. I've things to do." He pushed the door aside and strode out without another word.

Keturah's cheeks suddenly grew warm. She wiped at a tear forming in the corner of her eye and then got out of bed. She crossed her arms, staring at the closed door. It bothered her that he could be so insensitive, especially after she thought he might be making some amends. She'd only wanted to know where she could reach him.

And yet, she really shouldn't even care where he went or if he ever came back. He was hard to understand, and he didn't even seem to know what it was he wanted of her.

She pulled a wool scarf around her shoulders tightly and went into the other room.

A walk might do her good. It was a balmy, sunny day. She needn't let Joash's sullen moods destroy her own.

She turned to Joash's mother. "I'm going to Tirzah's." She adjusted the belt on her tunic and straightened. "I've not been to her house yet. But, won't be long, and I'll take one of the water jars to fill the cistern with."

Mary looked up. She was in front of the oven cleaning ashes out of it. "Take your time, Keturah. It's good to know she's living so close."

Keturah smiled. "Yes, I couldn't believe it. I only wish I would've known sooner." She took an empty water jug and hoisted it onto her shoulders. "I'll be back later."

Nissa came out of a back room and sat down next to her mother. She waved at Keturah.

Mary smiled. "Be careful."

Keturah smiled back. "I'll be fine." There would be no problem walking alone. It wasn't likely she'd have another incident such as she'd had with Nissa at the well. No one bothered her, once they found out who her husband was. Joash would have to understand she wouldn't be taking Nissa or his mother everywhere she went. She supposed most of the troubles were found deeper in the city, same as in Shiloh.

Keturah slipped out through the stone gate in the front of the home and took the hardened clay path to Tirzah's place. She walked along the side of the road.

The street was busy, today. There were many travelers heading in both directions. Some people were walking and carrying water jars like her. Some had baskets of supplies slung on their shoulders or were leading animals on ropes.

A New Dance

Wagons rolled past her, rocking back and forth on the uneven trail, either carrying things to the city to sell, or transporting building supplies or other materials.

Even though it was hot, there were some clouds in the sky dotting the horizon. Maybe later in the day, rain would come and cool things.

Keturah breathed in a sweet scent of lilies that floated past her, as she set her eyes on the road to where Tirzah's home was. It was a heavenly day, anything to take her mind from Joash and his troublesome behavior.

The country in Bethel wasn't much different than Shiloh. The vineyards covered the hills and valleys, dotting the countryside with lush, green leaves and large, purple grapes. She stopped a moment to watch the wooly sheep grazing in the fields and the shepherds carrying their staffs beside them, as they meandered over the hilltops. It was a peaceful, quiet scene, filling Keturah's heart with a pleasurable feeling.

The people on the road were friendly and helpful, pointing the way to Tirzah's home. Apparently, her friend made an impression on the people in the town. Everyone seemed to know where she lived.

She spotted the massive structure on the side of a hill where Tirzah's place was and started up the path toward it.

She wondered how her friend was doing. Tirzah didn't look unhappy the night of the festival. In fact, she seemed content and as if she accepted her home in Bethel rather favorably. She was glad her friend was faring so well.

She looked back down the road in the direction from where she'd come.

If only she could be so happy. She might even come to love Bethel like Shiloh.

She shook her head. Even though Bethel was beautiful and reminded her of home, everything was so very different here, especially when it came to Joash.

She kicked a small pebble out of the path, watching it roll under a shrub. She had to admit things had been better for whatever reason, at least until this morning. She could honestly say that this last time Joash had come home, she'd even found him bearable more times than not.

Her shoulder was tiring from the water jar, so she shifted it to the other side, adjusting the cloth draped on her head as she walked.

She stared at the hills in the distance. It was difficult to give herself fully to her husband, as he didn't make it easy.

Simeon told her to love his son, but she wondered how she could, when so many times he treated her as if she mattered so little. He also told her, Joash quit listening to the Lord a long time ago, and that if he'd only turn back, things might be different.

She let out a breath. His father had more confidence than she did, as she didn't see that happening anytime soon.

She looked up and smiled when she spotted her friend taking quick steps to greet her.

"Keturah!" Tirzah cried out. "How good to see you! I can't believe we're both here and together again."

She was beaming and looked very pretty in her light purple dress banded about her waist with a darker purple sash. The hem of her tunic was embroidered with tiny yellow flowers and fruit. She looked rich in her new attire.

Keturah eyed the tall, wide stone building that was Tirzah's home. "You're husband's done well." The outer walls were strong and well fortified. Hundreds of sheep grazed around it on the hillside, along a brook with trees on both banks.

"As everyone in this place has. I hear Joash isn't a poor man either."

"He has many things." Keturah's tone was dry. She sighed, taking her friend's arm and walking along next her in the courtyard, past a rounded stone oven near the house.

Tirzah eyed her curiously. "He's very handsome."

A look on consternation crossed Keturah's face, yet she nodded. "He does have some favorable qualities. And Bethel isn't so bad."

Tirzah smiled. "Yet, we're not in Shiloh, are we?"

"No. I wish we were closer. I'd love to see my family again."

Tirzah nodded. She had a wistful expression on her face. "Do you remember the night in the vineyards?"

Keturah sighed. "All I could think of was Shiloh, and my parents and brothers. I didn't understand what was happening. Life has changed so much."

Tirzah touched Keturah's arm. "Is it so bad?"

Keturah shrugged. "Leaving Shiloh? I think so."

"I know how much it meant to you, to make your life there."

A New Dance

She gestured for Keturah to follow her into the house. "Come. It's warm out here."

Tirzah led Keturah through the inner courtyard and to a stairway on a sidewall of her home. They went up the steps and into a room lit with oil lamps. "We'll have privacy here."

Keturah sat on a wide bench built into the wall, and Tirzah brought a container of water for them. She sat next to her friend and poured the clear liquid into cups and handed one to Keturah.

Keturah lifted the container to her lips, letting the cool drink refresh her after the long walk. "I'm really trying to understand why all this has happened."

Tirzah eyed her curiously, but didn't say anything.

Keturah stared out the arched doorway. She watched her friend get up and bring a lit oil lamp from a shelf against the wall and set it on the table.

Keturah sighed. "I only wonder why the Lord would send me to a place so far away, to be with a man I'm not sure how to love, when I prayed for so many years." Her eyes were dark and sad.

Tirzah sat back down. "I don't know what to say."

"Joash's father told me I was the answer to his prayer, but I can't see this." Keturah's brow wrinkled.

Tirzah reached out. "Oh, Keturah. We don't know what the Lord's final plan is. You know that he has one for you, and, that it is good."

Keturah shook her head, eying the flickering blaze on the wooden table bending and twisting into a myriad of colors. The glow from it permeated the small, dark cave-like structure where they sat. Life was like the flame, not knowing, what direction it would take.

Tirzah followed her gaze. "So many of God's people waited years for their promises to be fulfilled and were faithful, even when it did not seem as if the Lord was listening to them. But, he was." Tirzah smiled. "You can't give up on him. He has a plan for your life, Keturah."

Keturah nodded. "I want to believe it, but it's so difficult. If you knew the way Joash treated me, you'd understand why I'm wary. I've seen some good changes in him, yes. But, sometimes when I begin to think things are going better, they suddenly fall apart, like this morning. It was so unexpected. After spending a few almost pleasant days together, before he left, he turned back and looked at me, and it was as if I were dirt under his very feet. He left in a dark mood and wouldn't even answer when I called to him. He left no clue as to where he went and when he'd be back. He didn't even seem to care."

Tirzah sighed. "It surely can't be easy for you, Keturah. It's difficult to imagine anyone treating you that way." Tirzah played with the beads dangling from the fringe on her tunic. "And yet, maybe there are other reasons. With the position he holds in his tribe, he's most likely seen a lot of things we know nothing of and lived a harder life than most. Or maybe he's been hurt and has little trust. We might never know. But, we can't ever give up hope for others and must remember the Lord's promises to us."

Keturah sighed. "Simeon said to show his son love. To win him this way."

She pressed her lips together. "But, it's not so easy when he treats me the way he does, sometimes staring daggers at me, as if he can't stand the sight of me. It's times like these I don't want to be near him, let alone love him."

Tirzah took her hand. "I'm sorry. I suppose if I were in your place, my marriage would've been destroyed within the course of a week. The Lord knew what he was doing when he gave you Joash." She leaned closer. "You're a kind person, Keturah. And it is doubtless Joash has seen this, even if he hasn't shown it."

Keturah sighed. "I suppose I've not tried as hard as I could have. I've not been the person you knew back in Shiloh. Joash brings out in me a side you've not seen."

Tirzah wagged a finger at her. "But, you need to remember that his dark moods are not your fault. You mustn't ever blame yourself for his actions."

Keturah brightened a little and nodded. "I think that, too. Those things he does are not my responsibility, and I surely can't control any of it. But, I only wish I could curb my own temper. Even though I think he deserves every tongue-lashing he gets, it doesn't mean it's for the best. I should be able to respond in a better way than he does. Yet, most of the time, I feel like choking him instead."

Tirzah giggled mischievously at that. And then, she suddenly looked up, smiling, but not speaking.

Keturah knew that familiar twinkle her friend always got in her eye when she wanted to say something Keturah hardly ever agreed with.

124

"Tirzah?" She wasn't sure whether she wanted to hear what her friend had to say.

Tirzah's face brightened. "Do you ever wonder whether or not this situation might be *good* for you?"

"Good?" Keturah bristled, crossing her arms. Her brows shot up. "Living with Joash? I don't think you understand the extent of what I go through with him."

Tirzah grinned. "I might have an idea. I suppose from what you've told me, it's not easy, maybe like living with an ox?"

Keturah couldn't help laughing. "Aside from a temper and penchant for getting his own way, I think you might not be far from the truth.

"Well, I'm sure he'd be difficult for anyone to manage without a measure of help. So, do you see, that this could be a good thing?"

"I'm not sure what you're getting at." Keturah blinked, confused.

"Well, I think living with him has made you realize that there are some things you can't do in your own strength. In Shiloh, you were able to live your obedient life with little help from the Lord there. It was much easier, than here in Bethel."

Keturah released a breath. "You don't even know how difficult it's been with him."

Tirzah smiled. "With Joash, I suppose you need the Lord for help, as your ability to be obedient to Joash only goes so far on your own."

"More like it never seems to go anywhere." She thought a moment and then sighed, as if she knew where Tirzah was going with this. "But, I think I see. You believe I'm putting my trust in the Lord now, rather than in myself." She suddenly looked at Tirzah with a new understanding. "And because it is so, you believe my situation here might draw me closer to the Lord."

"Maybe."

Keturah bit her lip. "It is true that I've spent more time with the Lord here than I ever have before. With Joash, it's impossible not to."

Tirzah shrugged. "I learn more in my struggles, then in any other times. Our forefathers never led perfect lives. More than not, they were broken. Maybe you should consider your new husband a blessing."

"Joash?" Keturah stared at her friend, incredulous. The word blessing attached to him seemed preposterous. And then she smiled. "More like an Egyptian slave trader."

They both laughed.

But, maybe Tirzah was right? None of the forefathers had it easy. Joseph was sold into slavery. David was forced to hide in caves from enemies wanting to kill him. And there were countless others who had struggles of their own. Having the Lord in her life never was a promise of comfort or ease.

Tirzah smiled. "Even though Joash didn't make the decisions he did for good, the Lord made it a part of his plan. And *the Lord* is good, Keturah. We can count on that."

Keturah nodded.

Then Tirzah put her hand to her chest. She suddenly got a mischievous look in her eye. "And there might just be other reasons the Lord put you with Joash, you might consider."

Keturah shook her head. She knew her friend too well. "By the look on your face, I'm not sure the Lord has a lot to do with this idea, or that I want to hear it." But, she couldn't help smiling when she said it.

Tirzah giggled. "Well, maybe this wouldn't have come from the Lord, but I suppose anything is possible."

She tipped her head to the side. "I was thinking of how much you'd wish to share your dancing with the one you love someday. And the way I see it, I can't imagine Hiram appreciating your style of dance. Yet, something tells me Joash would not mind it at all. I suppose the Lord knew this, too."

"Tirzah!" Keturah felt her cheeks burn. She remembered what Joash once told her about her dancing. "You know my dance has always been for the Lord, like Miriam's. Not for either of *them*. And it wasn't meant to be for anything else."

Tirzah grinned, but her voice was soft. "I know that's true. But, so much of who we are and what makes us happy is best shared with our husbands. Someday, maybe Joash will appreciate this gift of yours."

Keturah sighed. "I'm sure it will never be something I would ever consider sharing with him. But, I suppose I can try to love him as his father wishes. Maybe this is what the Lord wants, too."

A New Dance

Tirzah's eyes sparkled. "Yes. And the Lord can teach you how. Keep your faith and prayers, and someday you'll see the purpose of your suffering."

Keturah leaned over and hugged Tirzah. "I knew there was a reason I needed to see you."

A low voice startled them both. "I see you've found your friend again." It was Isaac.

Tirzah practically flew to the door and took her husband's arm. "You're back early!"

Isaac smiled. "I'll be here today, but must finish my chores." He nodded to Keturah. "I just had to stop in a moment to give my regards."

Keturah smiled. "It's good to see you."

"Same here. I hope you and Tirzah enjoy your time together." He pushed on the handle of the door to leave again.

Tirzah let go of him. "I'll have a meal ready later." She watched him leave and then turned back to Keturah and sat back down on a mat on the floor.

They talked until late afternoon, and then Keturah left. She filled her water jug at a spring nearby and headed back to Joash's family's home.

Tirzah had given Keturah a lot to think about. Keturah resolved to not let her faith in the Lord waiver and to believe in his promises as her forefathers did.

*****

127

"And because iniquity shall abound, the love of many shall wax cold."
Matthew 24:12 King James's Version

Chapter 28

Keturah helped in the home, sewing, caring for the animals and making meals. Other times, she walked the paths of Bethel visiting Tirzah. It was wonderful getting reacquainted with her friend and a blessing to have someone to talk to.

She'd no clue as to when Joash would return. Mary said they never knew what to expect from him. But, in a way, Keturah liked the fact he was staying away as long as he had. There seemed to be less contention in the home when he was gone, and she felt more relaxed without him there.

Nissa was opening up to her, and they were becoming fast friends. Nissa even whispered to her once, so excited she was to tell Keturah news and had spoken to her in short sentences after that. Keturah didn't want to call attention to Nissa's shyness, so said nothing.

This afternoon, they were feeding the goats and stopped to rest.

Keturah pet a small, gray goat on the head, while she gave it food. "Which one do you like best?

Nissa pointed to a large black one and smiled.

Keturah nodded. "My Betsalel might be that big now. He was black, too."

Nissa said aloud. "I'm sorry Joash's horse had the same name." She looked at her lap.

Keturah was shocked to hear Nissa speak aloud, but said nothing.

She leaned over and threw more food on the ground for the goat. "Joash has a way of taking things that are mine." She looked solemn.

Nissa reached out and took Keturah's hand. Her voice was barely a whisper. "Don't be hard on him. I know he's difficult. But, it hasn't always been easy for him."

"Joash?" Keturah kept talking to Nissa as if she didn't notice anything out of the ordinary hearing her quiet voice and perfectly formed sentences. Joash was right. She did know how to talk. "Everything seems easy for him."

Nissa looked down at her lap. "Well, it hasn't been."

"Yet, I can't feel sorry for him or for anything that's happened in his life. I'm sure he deserved every bit of it."

Nissa took her arm. She suddenly spoke without timidity. "But, I think he treats you this way, because of things that happened to him in the past."

Keturah looked genuinely interested.

Nissa played with the folds of her skirt. She seemed unsure whether or not to continue. "When he was younger, there was this woman named Deborah in his life, and he loved her very much."

"Joash? What happened to her? Why isn't she with him?"

Nissa whispered close to Keturah's ear. "He thought she was going to marry him, but in the end she chose someone else. He used to talk to me, because he knew I wouldn't say anything. She was very beautiful and made him believe they would be together, but it didn't happen. He's not trusted any other woman since."

Keturah got up and spread grain on the ground, contemplating this new bit of information. His behavior toward her made more sense.

Nissa went to her and kissed her on the cheek. "I'm happy you're here now."

Keturah hugged her and took her hand. "And I'm glad I know you." She smiled. "I appreciate you telling me this. I'll try and show your brother kindness."

She took another handful of grain from her sack and went back to work.

They finished in the courtyard, then cleaned up and went inside.

Keturah went to a window and looked out, watching the hills for a lone rider, but seeing none. She wondered where Joash was and what he was doing. Maybe over time, he'd see that she was different, and something might change between them.

***

Joash stared into the fire, sitting in the camp. "I'm not sure how to deal with Keturah."

Daniel eyed him curiously. "Why?"

Joash shrugged. "I don't know. But, maybe she expects too much from me."

"She's your wife."

Joash frowned. "I've given her a home, many fine animals and clothes. She likes my family. What else is there?"

Daniel stirred the fire, making the flames grow higher. "Does she know you love her?"

Joash grunted. "I took her to the festival and did things to show her how I feel."

"But, did you tell her you love her?" Daniel looked serious.

Joash poked at the flames with a stick, annoyed at the turn of the conversation. After loving Deborah and losing her, something in him seemed to die. And then he went to war and with each battle, he seemed to grow colder and harder. How could he even know how to open up to someone again?

"I'm not sure that's possible for me."

Daniel smiled. "I think with the Lord, it would be." He patted Joash's arm. "Just pray. And let him show you how."

Joash eyed the dying embers of the fire and scraped the charred rocks around it with a stick. "I'm not sure I can do that, either."

Yet, he puzzled over the fact that these same thoughts kept coming to him, that he should turn back in that direction.

So far he'd failed at just about everything he did in regards to Keturah. His father and Daniel were not experiencing the same with their wives. Maybe, it was time to listen and put his trust in the Lord's guidance, rather than trying in his own strength and failing.

***

Joash rode in front of the group of men. He held his sling at his side and readied himself. His expression was grim and his body tense. He was prepared for this type of combat, something he knew how to do.

He pushed Betsalel faster. The dust was rising behind the horses, and he calculated from it how many were coming. He moved with the horse charging across the fields.

Keturah became a hazy memory, and the reality of his life was in front of him. He understood the cries of battle and wounds of victory.

It was here he felt most alive, fighting against other men. In this place there was never any middle ground. He knew what to do.

***

It'd been months since Joash had been home. Keturah was walking back from Tirzah's home, as had been her routine, when she moved to the side of the street, at the sound of horse's hooves behind her. She turned when she realized Joash was back home.

She wanted to run to him and welcome him home, but then backed up a step. There was a dark look on his face.

He got off the horse and went to her, grabbing hold of her arm and swinging her around. "What're you doing?"

Right away, Keturah lost all compassion she had for him.

She shook her arm free. "And why should I answer to that, when you're never here!" She pushed him away and began walking the path. She felt hot tears coming to her eyes.

Joash stared at her crossly. "Because, I'm you're husband." His voice was a command.

Keturah stopped, turning around, her eyes glittering. "And you're greeting me this way, after being gone so long?" Her hands shook, and she had to hold them to her side. "I was at Tirzah's, if you must know!"

She turned from him, holding her face in her hands and began to weep. "What do you want? What do I have to do to be acceptable to you?"

He let out an exasperated sound, yet his expression softened as he loosened his hold on her. He looked as if he were conflicted. "Stay on the main road from now on."

Keturah stared at him indifferently through tear-stained eyes. And then she reached out and touched the side of his face. "I was waiting for you to come back."

His eyes narrowed, and he waved her hand off. He made a sound, and took his horse by the reigns and began walking away.

Her voice was almost a whisper, as she trailed after him. "I won't be unfaithful, Joash, like Deborah."

He turned around. There was heat in his face.

She stopped and looked anxiously at her feet.

"The only one who knew about her was Nissa?"

Keturah lifted her eyes to his and nodded.

His brow curled, and he scrutinized her. "But, she doesn't talk."

"Not to you. But, I wouldn't either, if you were my brother. I'm sure you scare her."

He stared at her, puzzled, with an astonished look on his face. "What else did she say?"

She looked at her feet, hesitant.

"Tell me. What was it?"

She lifted her chin, a spark in her eye, as she looked directly at him. "She told me much about what you told her. And spoke very well. But, the last thing she said, was that, you reminded her a mule. And I think, it is not far from the truth."

She smiled at his dumbfounded expression, as she left him behind strolling ahead to the house, a small triumph for having to deal with his return.

*****

"They shall run like mighty men; they shall climb the wall like mighty men of war; and they shall march every one on his ways, and they shall not break their ranks:" Joel 2:7 King James's Version

Chapter 29

Joash came to dinner, dressed in a clean robe and sandals.

Nissa leaned close to Keturah in the courtyard next to the stone oven, whispering in her ear when he came through the door.

Nissa's eyes were shining as she ran up to throw her arms around him. "Brother." She whispered it his ear.

His regarded her with an astonished expression and picked her up swinging her into his arms. "What's happened to you?" He set her back down, going to where Keturah was taking bread from the rounded, stone oven.

"How did you do it?" He looked bewildered.

She pushed him back out of the way, pulling the bread out with a flat tool. "Move. Or it'll be ruined."

Nissa started to giggle behind them

Keturah placed the loaf on the ledge of a stone block to cool and turned around. "I didn't do anything. No one would have responded well to you. Like I said before, with you as a brother, I'm sure I wouldn't have ever spoken."

He took the wooden tool from her hands and set it against the house. Then he took her in his arms and leaned down and kissed her, more persistently than he'd ever done.

She felt the breath go out of her, and when he set her away from him, she stared at him, trying to figure out what just happened.

He seemed to be watching what her reaction to him would be. He looked entertained by the emotions playing out in her face.

She felt confused, and her cheeks burned at the thought of him kissing her in the courtyard in front of Nissa.

"Nissa, we have to finish the meal. And your brother has chores to do." She pulled Nissa into the house and could hear laughter in the courtyard.

She shook her head, not sure what to think.

***

Keturah went outside after the meal and sat on the stone steps, watching the sun go down. Joash could have some time to talk to his parents. He seemed in a better mood than usual, and she wasn't sure why, but suspected it had something to do with Nissa.

She wondered what her own family was doing in Shiloh. She'd love to see her mother and father again, and her brothers. What would her life have been like, if she were still at home?

***

Joash stood next to his father, looking out over the land. The vineyards were full with lush grapes and needed to be taken care of. The still evening air was cool, and the night was drawing closer. Crickets were singing, and there were the low braying sounds of the animals in the stables.

What he was going to tell his father would impact him greatly. He spoke quietly with conviction. "I'm praying now, father."

Simeon took his son's arm. He turned, bewildered. "What?"

Joash shrugged. "I've been speaking with the Lord."

Simeon stared, openmouthed. "Oh. How did this come about?"

"Daniel and I talked. I decided to make changes, if it's possible."

Simeon let out a breath. "Oh, son, we all need the Lord's guidance. You'll find things better with him."

Joash tore off a piece of wheat and chewed on the end. "I'm hoping. But, of course, I've already failed once. The first thing I did when I got back was yell at Keturah. I lose my temper so easily, and I know she doesn't deserve it."

His father patted his arm and smiled. "Old habits take time to change."

"I suppose."

"The fact, that you feel for what you've done is the first step. I've seen little of that in you before, so it shows that the Lord's already changing you."

Joash looked at his father. "That's good to hear. I never thought of it that way."

A New Dance

And then he took a deep breath. "So, why has it taken me so long to realize I needed the Him? Why wouldn't I listen?"

Simeon shook his head. "The Lord's good, Joash. He knew when to speak to you in his own way and time. I've been praying a long time for this."

Joash nodded. His heart lightened inside with the thought that his father had persisted.

***

Keturah took a seat in the courtyard by Nissa on a woven mat. She started stitching the edge of a new brown robe for Joash. But, before she could get more than a couple stitches finished, he came in through the door.

She looked down, hoping he'd pass by, but realized she wasn't so lucky when his sandaled feet stopped in front of her.

"Come and walk with me."

Keturah spoke softly. "I have to finish this."

He leaned down and placed the garment she was working on to the side. "I've many robes."

Nissa's face lit. "I'll finish it."

Keturah frowned at her.

Nissa took Joash's robe, laying it across her lap. She smiled.

Joash grasped Keturah's hand and pulled her to her feet.

"But, we've work to do." Keturah took a step back.

"It'll wait. You can do it when you get back. I want to spend time with you."

"You're not going to the city?"

"No." He looked out of the courtyard. "You've never seen our land and where the boundaries lie. I want you to see what's yours."

Keturah eyed him suspiciously. "But, why?"

He had an odd expression on his face, almost as if he didn't know what to say. And then he shrugged. "I don't know. Father wanted me to show you."

"Oh."

Keturah walked next to him in silence, every now and then glancing at him, trying to figure out what was different about him.

He kept hold of her hand as they walked. Strangely enough, he did as he said he would and took her around the property, pointing out the boundaries.

Keturah relaxed when she realized he had no other motive. "What's this place?"

He put his hand against a cliff-like structure. "I used to play here as a child. We'd see who could get to the top first."

She eyed his strong-looking arms. "And I suppose you were usually first?" She remembered what his father had told her.

"I was." She was surprised he almost looked sad when he said it. "Someone had to be."

She put her hand on the rock, gripping one of the crevices. "Could you take me up there? Show me how to do it?"

"You?" Joash laughed, and then realized she was intent on it. He shook his head. "No."

"But why not? I know I could do it."

He was serious, but had a smile on his face.

She sighed. "Please. You don't have to tell anyone. It's not high. And I want to see what's up there."

"But, you're a woman."

She took him by the arms, her expression hopeful. "Please…"

Joash hesitated a second. The look in his face was an odd mix. And then he let out a breath. "Mother won't be happy with me if anything happens to you."

She laughed. "You'll do it?" She reached out, leaning forward, and she took his arm.

He nodded reluctantly. "I shouldn't, but…"

Keturah's eyes glowed. "Come. Show me."

He let out a breath. "Fine."

She clasped her hands in front of her. A feeling of anticipation welled up inside of her.

He took her hand and placed it on the wall. Then he cautioned, "Here, watch what I do and put your feet in the same cracks I put mine in. Follow my lead and lean against the wall. And don't look down."

"Height doesn't bother me."

He looked at her amused. He turned to the wall and searched for a strong crevice to put his foot in, boosting himself up.

Keturah followed, mimicking his actions. She found it was easier than she thought it would be, but it did take some strength. She followed his lead, until they reached the last ledge. She was getting tired, but was thrilled at what she was doing.

Joash made the last move and crawled up over the wall, eying her with fascination as she put her foot in the last crevice.

When she reached the top, he helped her over. She sat down next to him and looked over the valley. The view was breathtaking. She smiled with satisfaction over her small accomplishment.

"I see I was wrong." He grinned.

Keturah nodded. "It wasn't so difficult." She drew in a breath as she eyed the rolling hills in the distance beneath blue skies. "It's beautiful."

He didn't take his eyes from her, nodding.

***

They stayed for a time, and he showed her the quickest way to get down.

When they reached the bottom, he spoke quietly. "We've been longer than I thought."

He took her hand and she walked with him, watching the path.

She stopped to pick some flowers on the way back and then got down by a spring near the house to drink water.

She cupped her hands, filling them, with the clear, cool liquid. She lifted the water to her mouth, letting it trickle down her throat, then looked at the bouquet. "I'll put them in a jar inside."

Joash smiled, as if amused. "We can see them outside anytime we like. Why are you bringing them in the house?"

She made a face. "Why do you think?"

"I've no idea." He picked up the flowers and handed them to her. "Here, do with them as you please. But if we wait too long, we'll miss the meal."

Keturah went ahead of him to Simeon, who was waiting at the gate. They stepped through and went into the house. Mary and Nissa had dinner ready.

***

A few months had gone by and Keturah stood looking over the horizon. Deep purple flowers filled the valley and trails of oranges and yellows flooded the sky as the sun sunk beneath the earth. She let out a breath at the beauty of it and prayed a prayer that the Lord would continue to show her the wonders he'd created.

She felt hands on her shoulders and turned. Her eyes were drawn upward.

Joash bent to kiss her, his expression tender.

Keturah was confused by the changes in him. Since he'd come home, he'd been treating her differently, and she didn't quite understand what had come over him. She almost felt as if he was beginning to care for her, but was afraid to believe it.

Seeing the changes, she couldn't deny the feelings she began to have for him. She hoped she wouldn't be sorry for allowing herself to trust a man who might hurt her in the end.

***

Keturah woke early the next morning and got up. She could see out a small window high on the wall where a shaft of light found it's way in the room. The sky was blue, and it looked like it was going to be another good day.

She wrapped a scarf around her shoulders after donning a new tunic and then looked around the room for her sandals. Now, where did she put them?

When she turned, she noticed Joash eying her from where he lay. He got up and went to her, putting his hand near her waist. He had a curious look in his eyes.

She turned to him puzzled. "What?"

"You're still not with child?" And then he frowned. "Shouldn't it have happened by now?"

She moved away. "Joash, no one can know when that will happen. You can't will these things, yourself. Now, leave me. I need to find my sandals." She looked around the floor and spotted them in a corner.

She went to get them, but he took her by the elbow and turned her back.

He looked impatient. "It's only, we've few men in our tribe. We need heirs. It's important to the Benjamites."

"But, I've no control over that. I already told you. No one does, except the Lord."

Joash sighed. "But, it's why…" And then he stopped.

"Why what?"

He reached for her, but she backed away from him.

Something sick churned inside her as she eyed him warily. "Why you took me from my home and family? I remember what you said." Her eyes narrowed.

She suddenly was beginning to understand his behavior toward her and his wanting to spend so much time with her.

"You know what I meant." He went over to a bench at the other end of the room and took a clean striped robe and slipped it over his head. Then he turned to her as he tied a leather belt around his waist. "It means a lot to me."

Keturah felt the ire rising inside her. Of all the things. He made her believe he cared for her.

Joash laughed. "Now, you're upset."

She went to the corner of the room and grabbed her sandals and took them to the bed. She began wrapping the leather straps around her ankles and tying the tops.

He crossed the room.

"Don't." She put out her hand as if to stop him. "I'm going out."

Joash took her by the arms and pulled her to him. His eyes glittered dangerously. "You'll stay and talk to me."

She pushed him off and went to the door. "No."

But, before she left, she turned around. "What if I'm unable to have a child? What then?" She knew what women meant to him. "You'll take a concubine or another wife, a foreign woman?"

He hesitated a little too long.

"You would. Wouldn't you?" She rubbed her temples. It was all making sense to her, now.

"Keturah, you're my wife. You'll have a child with me. Our baby."

Keturah felt heat rising inside her. She fumed, as she looked into his cool, dark eyes. Why didn't she see any of this before?

She should've known there was another motive for all the care he'd taken the last months. People just didn't change that suddenly. Had she forgotten what he was like before?

It was clear to her, he hadn't.

Kara S. McKenzie

She choked back a sob and turned so he wouldn't see. "I have to get the morning meal started. I need to go."

She heard no response from him and went into the next room, getting a sack of barley from the shelf and other ingredients. She took them out the door and into the courtyard. After making a fire in the oven, she ground the barley in a wooden bowl, while she sat on the porch.

She looked at the entrance to the home, suddenly feeling sick. She stirred the rest of the ingredients together.

Tears flooded her eyes, but she brushed them off her cheeks. An ached settled deep inside her. She remembered back to the time he said he wasn't able to love her the way she wanted, that he only wanted a child.

She suddenly wanted to leave, to find a way back to her home, far from Bethel. She was beginning to have feelings for him. This couldn't happen.

As she kneaded the bread dough in the bowl, shaping it into a loaf, she looked out over the horizon, her eyes seeking the hills in the distance.

If she left him, Joash would be disgraced. He might not even come for her, if she wounded his pride. Her father would surely keep him from her. Then, it'd all be over.

But she'd have to find a way out of this city and home first. And do it in a way he wouldn't suspect.

She set the bowl down and covered it with a cloth, and cleared the hot coals from the oven, using a tool to put the loaves inside. She sat back down on the porch, listening to the bawl of a camel in the gated area near the house. If she could just get on the next caravan.

She'd talk to Tirzah. Tirzah's husband would know when the next group was leaving and who would be on it. She was sure there hadn't been one going that way for a long time, so there would be one leaving soon. She'd to talk to Tirzah as soon as Joash left again and would find out what she needed to know.

*****

140

"I would hasten my escape from the windy storm and tempest." Psalm 55:8 King James's Version

Chapter 30

"You're going with Isaac to Shiloh?"

Keturah sat on the long wooden bench in the courtyard next to her friend. She couldn't believe what she was hearing. "Please, Tirzah. Take me with you. I can't stay here longer. I don't want to be here."

Tirzah put down the basket she was working on and smoothed back Keturah's hair. "I'll ask."

Keturah frowned. "But, Isaac won't do it. Please Tirzah. What can we do?"

"I'll tell Isaac you've Joash's permission. He'd take you, then."

"Oh, Tirzah. I could never make it to Shiloh by myself. There'd be no other way. And I want to be with my parents." Keturah's heart leapt in her chest.

"But, you know Joash will go after you. He'll know where you're headed."

"I know. But, if he does, I also know my father won't make me go back with him, when he knows what Joash is like. We haven't been married long."

Tirzah put her arms around Keturah. "It must be terrible for you to do something like this. You're the last one I'd suspect such a thing."

"I don't know what else to do."

Tirzah picked the basket back up and wove a long reed through the top of the container. "We'll take you. But, you must be ready, as we're heading out the day after next Sabbath."

Keturah shook her head. "I'll get my things together and come then. He left a short time ago, and he'll be gone for at least a month."

"Good. We'll leave at dawn."

***

On the morning of their allotted departure, Nissa was up early, too. When Keturah tiptoed across the courtyard, she stopped short.

"What are you doing?" Nissa got up from the bench she was sitting on.

Keturah put her hand to her chest. "Nissa. I'm sorry." Tears flooded her eyes. "I'm going to Shiloh."

"What?" Nissa practically jumped back an arm's length. "But, you can't."

"I have to, Nissa. It might've worked if Joash cared for me, but I don't see it."

Nissa looked concerned. "I think he does, Keturah. I think he's changed."

"He wants a baby, to carry on the name. He so much as said he would take other wives. And I couldn't have that."

"Joash? Said that?" She looked surprised. "But what will you do? And what if he goes after you?"

"I'll be with my parents." Keturah looked pained. "My father will convince him to divorce. There are other women."

Nissa begged her. "Divorce? No. Please. I know he loves you. Give him a chance. You can't do this."

"I'm sorry. But, I have to leave. Tirzah and her husband are waiting."

Nissa threw her arms around Keturah. "Oh. I've grown to love you so."

Tears came to Keturah's eyes. "I love you also, and your parents. I wish it could be another way. But, we'll still be sisters. It doesn't matter where we live."

She turned and went out the doorway, heartbroken to be leaving Nissa, but determined.

***

Traveling was slow, but Keturah was comforted by the fact that Joash would be gone months and wouldn't discover her missing until she was already in Shiloh. Her heart lifted at the thought of seeing her beloved home. It wouldn't be long, before they'd be there. The hills rose up in the distance, the sun spraying light over the tops.

Tirzah smiled as they walked the path, alongside the donkey. "You're brave to leave him. He's a man even I wouldn't dare to cross."

Keturah sighed. She didn't deny the trepidation she felt inside when she thought of what Joash would do when he found out she was gone. But, once she was safe at her father's home, he could do nothing. Her mother and father would listen to her and not allow him to come near her.

"He'll get over this. I'm not going back with him."

"But, if your father convinces him to divorce you, you'll be looked down upon. Everyone will despise you, and you'll not have any friends. Do you know what it'll be like?"

"My parents will not despise me. I know it. Nor my brothers. And of course, Betsalel."

Tirzah laughed. "That goat. Such a silly thing."

Keturah smiled. "Yes." And then she spotted the path ahead that led into her village. "Shiloh!" Her breath came out in gasps. "Home!"

***

Keturah stood at the edge of her parent's place, staring at it, as if in a dream. Her mother was in the courtyard behind the stone gate.

"Mother! I'm home!" She ran through the gate and into comforting arms and fell to weeping.

Her mother looked confused. "My dearest. What are you doing here? Where's your husband, the Benjamite?"

Keturah couldn't quit crying for the joy of being home with family again. Her brothers and father came out of the house and joined them, each one taking their turn and hugging her.

She knelt down on the ground and put her head in her hands. She spoke quietly. "I've left him."

The courtyard was silent as a tomb other than the sound of the crackle of fire in the oven next to them. Keturah looked up, waiting for one of them to answer.

Her brothers just stared at her openmouthed.

Her mother was silent.

"Keturah." Her father's brow rose. "You can't leave your husband."

Her mother got up, her face pale. She was staring at Keturah as if she'd seen an apparition. She clutched her chest. "Is he so bad?"

Keturah stood, taking a step back. She looked down at her feet and twisted her tunic in her hands. She'd seen changes for the better in Joash, but she didn't want to go back to him. She had to convince her parents that he wasn't a good man. If he came looking for her, they'd surely see evidence of his explosive nature. He wouldn't accept things meekly.

"Mother, he has no love for me. He hasn't been kind." She wiped tears that kept dropping from her cheeks. "I tried, but I'm nothing to him."

Her father went to her and tipped up her chin. "It can't be true. You're beautiful, a good, obedient girl. He must see this."

The look in Caleb's eyes was incredulous. "She can't do this. Our family will be ruined. Despised."

Her mother sat down on a flat stone against the wall. She was still holding her chest. "Keturah, are you sure you can't go back to him, if he'll take you? Think about what you're doing. I know you love Shiloh, but…"

Keturah stood to her feet and wrapped her shawl around her body tighter. She was spent and suddenly was dizzy, and spun inside like she was going to be sick. She felt herself falling to the ground, but not before her father caught her in his arms.

She could see his face, but everything was foggy, and his voice slowed and sounded lower, until she slipped away.

*****

"For this cause shall a man leave his mother and father, and cleave to his wife." Mark 10:7 King James's Version

Chapter 31

Keturah woke, feeling slightly queasy. The moment she lifted her head, she began to wretch in the wooden container next to her bed. The room she was in was small and cavernous, lit by a small lamp, atop a wooden shelf on the wall. She couldn't see anything very well, other than the opening to the room and the small flame letting off little light.

Her mother was sitting by her side, holding a cool compress over her brow. "You're awake. I think this was all very much for you."

Keturah nodded. "I don't feel so well." She still was somewhat dizzy. Even though she was hungry, she didn't think she'd be able to keep any food down if she tried eating, so she didn't ask for it.

Her mother touched her shoulder. "You'll be fine. With a little rest." Her cheeks were rosy. "There's something I need to tell you."

Keturah turned away. Fear edged its way through her, as she lifted her hands to her middle. She raised her hands to her ears as if to block out what her mother was going to say. She couldn't hear this, as she knew it would create problems with Joash.

"It is true. You're with child."

Keturah made a sound. She lowered her hands and choked back a soft cry.

Her mother patted her arm. "The babe is on its way." She wet the cloth again in a large bowl with water in it and wrung it out, placing it back over Keturah's head. "You have to eat."

Keturah grew pensive.

Her mother looked worried. "What?"

"He'll not let me go." Keturah looked pained. "When he knows about the child, he'll want me back."

Her mother placed a hand on her daughter's arm. "Oh."

Keturah whispered. "Please don't tell father or brothers. None of them can know. Joash will never let me leave him if he finds out."

Her mother straightened. "But, Keturah. Then, you'll be divorced with a child. Could you bear such a disgrace? Could you put that on your brothers, who are still looking for wives?"

Keturah groaned. "Please, mother. Don't say anything, until I know what to do. I can't go back with him. I don't know what's to become of me. I want to stay in Shiloh."

She leaned over and wretched again into the container, pulling her hair back from her shoulders.

Keturah lay back down, looking up at the ceiling in the dark, lamp-lit room. "Please, I need to be alone. I'm sorry for the trouble I'm causing."

Her mother leaned over her. "You've done nothing, dearest. I don't know why our Lord has allowed such a thing, but there's certainly a reason. You've always been a good daughter. I don't understand such suffering."

"At one time, I found myself beginning to care for him, mother. But, he didn't love me." She put her hands to her face.

Her mother groaned. "Oh, my poor darling." She took her into her arms.

Keturah wiped tears that fell in a steady stream. She held her hand to her abdomen. "Please tell this to no one."

Her mother nodded, her expression full of compassion. "I won't." She got up and went to the door, looking back once and then going into the next room.

The secret would be safe. Keturah and her mother would keep it that way. She was secure in this, until they knew what to do.

* * *

Tirzah said goodbye to Keturah. She and her husband joined the caravan and headed out. Keturah ached that she might never see her friend again. She was sure they wouldn't be traveling back this way. The journey was dangerous and unpredictable and not one they'd wish to keep making. Tirzah's parents were pleased with Isaac and glad to see their daughter happy.

Keturah raised her hand one last time. "Bye." She whispered the words, an ache settling deep inside her as she forlornly watched the caravan move out of the village and into the distance, until they were no more.

Keturah walked back to her parent's home and into the courtyard. Her brother Caleb raised silent eyes to her. She felt shunned,

even by the family who once loved her. All but her mother, sided with
Joash.

***

"Where is she?" Joash shouted it to no one in particular.
"Someone knows what's happened to her, and I'm going to find out."
He stormed through the house, knocking down anything in the way.

His father followed behind him. "Joash, get ahold of yourself.
What did you do to make her leave? I thought you were making
changes?"

Joash flung Keturah's clothes aside. "I was. I don't know. She
went to Shiloh, didn't she?" He'd do anything to get his hands on her
right now. She'd pay dearly for the trouble she caused.

His father put up his hand. "Joash, if you go there acting like
this, you better watch out, or you'll lose her."

Joash slammed his fist on a stand next to him. "But, she's my
wife, father." He let out a groan. "She'll come back, if I have to drag
her back with me." He looked as if he were beside himself.

"If she is with her father as I suspect, and you go there in this
state of mind, he'll not let you near her. Her family is close."

Joash sat down on a slab of carved stone and sunk his head into
his hands. He never imagined she'd leave. He was sick inside. What
made her go? Hadn't she noticed the changes in him?

And now, he had to take off after her.

His horse needed a rest, but tomorrow morning, he'd head out.
After that, he wouldn't wait any longer.

His father laid a hand on Joash's shoulder. "Be good to her.
She's deserved none of what she's gotten."

Joash looked directly at his father. "I've been praying, father. I
don't understand what happened, or what I did to make her leave. It's a
misunderstanding."

He let out a quiet breath, shaking his head. "I'll to pray to the
Lord and listen and do his will in this."

Simeon's eyes glistened with tears. He choked on his next
words. "May you come back with your wife, and may the Lord bless
your life and Keturah's."

Joash left his father and went out into the night, looking up at
the stars, which spread their lights across the heavens.

"Be with me." He let out a breath, closing his eyes and clasping his hands. "Let me have a second chance with her. Help me to make things right. Lead me to do what you want. Show me what she needs."

Tears stained his cheeks, and he wiped them away.

"Joash." There was a sound behind him. He turned.

Nissa was standing in the shadows.

"Come." He motioned her to draw nearer. "Here."

Nissa edged nearer to him. She pulled her shawl around her shoulders and stood there quietly. "So, you're commanding me, rather than asking?"

His eyes narrowed, and then he eyed her impish smile and let out a breath. "You, too? It seems no one's pleased with me lately. I think Keturah's the one who's stole all your hearts."

She went to him and put her hand on his arm. "I love you, brother. I always have."

Her warmth and gentle words struck him deep in his heart. He was ashamed at the way he'd treated her in the past. He never noticed the sweetness in her or realized what a beautiful person she was, until Keturah was able to bring this side of her out. He only saw what he thought was important, but didn't realize the brokenness that was in him.

Sorrow penetrated his heart. "I've done so much wrong. I've made so many mistakes." He sighed. "I'm sorry, Nissa."

Nissa let go and smoothed back his hair. She smiled. "You command soldiers as your job. And you're very good at it. It's what you need to do on the battlefield." She smiled. "But, you must remember that at home, you can't always expect the same out of us."

The air was cool, and the sounds of crickets and night birds, were like a quiet melody under heaven's canopy. Joash looked at Nissa imploring her. "Did she tell you anything about me?"

Nissa grew quiet. "Not much. But, when she looked at you, I know she liked what she saw."

He studied her, curious. "She said this?"

"No, but I could tell." She looked away. "But, many women look at you that way."

Joash shrugged. "What else did she say?"

Nissa seemed as if she didn't want to tell him. "Not much." She put her hand on his shoulder.

"What?"

"She thought you could never love her, that you were incapable. But, I think you want to."

He sighed. "Maybe, I can't. Not the way she wants. I understand little of this."

She smiled. "Women are different than soldiers. You only have to figure them out."

He let out a painful sounding laugh. Then, he bent closer. "You said she told you a couple things about me. What else?"

She smiled pursing her lips and shook her head.

He took her arm and started tickling her. "Tell me. I want to know. And I won't stop until you do."

He tormented her, until her giggles were in fits, and she put out her hand for him to stop. "All right, all right." She spoke between breaths. "I'll say it."

He laughed, curious.

Nissa caught her breath. "You wanted to know."

He nodded.

"She said you were like the donkey, always braying and being ridiculous, what we were laughing about when you came in the courtyard that day."

"But, she told me *you* were the one who said I was like that?"

She smiled. "Well, we both did. But, she said the part about braying."

He let out a light chuckle and smiled. "I suppose I can't blame her."

Her eyes lit. "You can change and convince her of your love for her." She got up. "Then, she'll come back."

She put her hand on his shoulder. "But, you have to get to sleep first, if you leave tomorrow. And I should, too. You've a long trip ahead. Put your trust in the Lord. I'll pray for you."

Joash watched her leave, and then looked into the night.

Keturah was out there somewhere, miles from him.

He pushed his hands through his hair, frustrated. He'd some work ahead of him. He shook his head, wondering if he could ever convince her of the changes he planned to make. And he wondered if it were possible. He'd failed so much in the past. Could the Lord change his future?

149

He got up and followed Nissa out the door and made his way to the back to the soft pallet so that he could lie down for the night. Morning would come soon enough.

*****

"But every vow of a widow, and of her that is divorced, wherewith they have bound their souls, shall stand against her." Numbers 30:9 King James's Version

Chapter 32

Keturah stayed in her parent's home most of the time keeping out of sight from curious eyes. She helped her mother with chores, preparing meals and making clothing for the baby she carried within her.

She rubbed her abdomen, thinking of the new life growing inside her and smiled. Some good did come from difficult circumstances.

The room held a soft glow from the sunshine spilling in through the small window in the room. The summer light warmed her, and she suddenly wanted to be outside in it.

She put on the lavender tunic she made before she was taken to Bethel. It felt light and soft against her skin. She tied a darker purple belt around her waist and took a shawl with her to throw over her shoulders.

No one was home today. No one would notice her missing.

She peeked into the courtyard and didn't see anyone, so she tiptoed out and around the corner, taking Betsalel with her.

***

Joash's eyes narrowed. Keturah was sneaking out of her parent's home.

His heart raced at the sight of her leading the small, black goat out into the meadow.

Who did she plan to meet?

He crept along the path, watching her skip down the narrow road that lead to a small hillside tucked away from the city. He'd never seen her so carefree.

She was as beautiful as he remembered, her dark hair falling in waves down her back and her eyes wide and full of spirit.

When she came to a meadow dipping out of sight from the homes in Shiloh, she sat down on the ground and began removing her sandals.

Joash scanned the area for anyone who might be joining her, but found none.

When she got up, she was barefoot. She released the scarf from her shoulders and held it in her hands. She began twirling it in front of her, swaying to the rhythm of the light breeze. She lifted her face to the sunbeams stretching out to greet her and began to dance.

He couldn't take his eyes from her, fascinated by the way her body moved in perfect cadence to the nature around her.

He remembered back to the first time he saw her and felt the same attraction to her he had then, but now felt it only stronger. She was lovely in her soft, lavender tunic moving with her in gentle waves.

At that moment, he wished to know everything there was about her, her hopes and dreams and secret desires and how he could make her happy. He wanted her back with him, so that he could love her like she deserved. And he hoped to gain her love, which he knew was something he was willing to fight for.

***

When Keturah finished dancing, she stood looking out over the hills of Shiloh. She couldn't begin to describe the beauty of the place.

The vineyards were ripe with purple grapes coloring the valley. The sky was as blue as Bethel, meeting the green, rocky hills below. She stood amazed, as she wrapped her scarf back around her shoulders.

"You're beautiful." There was voice behind her, as a hand slid over her waist and tightened around her.

Joash. She closed her eyes. He came for her? She was prepared for him though and knew what she was going to say.

But before she could get a word out, his hand moved along her waist, and he whispered in her ear. "A child."

Keturah sucked in a breath, as he turned her to him.

"It's not true." She frowned and pulled away.

His eyes narrowed, and he studied her in earnest. Then, they landed on her thickening middle, and he smiled.

She turned from him. "No."

Then he laughed, and she shook her head, pursing her lips into a hard line. He was still the same man that she left back in Bethel, and she wanted no part of him. The child was the only thing he cared about.

He caught her around the waist again and breathed low into her ear. "You're carrying my baby."

She felt a heated, anger deep inside her. She didn't like how he treated her and how he made her feel, like a possession or prize, something he could control and use when desired.

She turned in his arms and shoved at his chest, pushing him away. Her dark eyes were flashing, and she lifted her chin high. "My father will make you divorce me."

*****

"Ask me never so much dowry and gift, and I will give according as ye shall say unto me; but give me the damsel to wife." Genesis 34:12 King James's Version

Chapter 33

Keturah grabbed her sandals and stormed away from him toward her home.

Joash was boiling inside, and it took all he had to not charge after her and demand that she come back with him. He stopped for a moment to say a quick prayer to keep composed and wait to know what to do. He figured it wouldn't help the matter to go back to his old ways.

He couldn't believe what she just told him, that she'd choose to spend the rest of her life as a divorced woman with a child, rather than go home with him. She'd surely be scorned by others, possibly even her own family and treated as if she were no better than dust under their feet until the day she died. And there'd be no possibility of any man considering marriage to her, ever.

This was how much she despised him and was willing to rid herself of him. And he had thought she was beginning to care for him. But, apparently she'd been hiding her true feelings all along.

He looked down the path where she'd fled and shook his head. He had to get ahold of himself and do things differently if he ever wanted a chance to be with her again.

He dropped down on his knees and bowed his head. "Oh, Lord. Forgive me for what I've done, and tell me what to do. Help me understand your will in this." And he knew, that nothing in these plans included a divorce.

***

Joash stared at the mud-brick home with the rock-strewn entrance leading into the courtyard. Keturah's small, black goat was bleating next to the home, and there was a fire in the oven. He smoothed the side of his robe and shook his hands in a nervous gesture as he neared the gate. It was the most difficult thing for him to do, to stand there calmly and make his way to the house.

A New Dance

He had time to cool down and think about how he should present himself to Keturah's parents. He needed to take his father's advice this time.

If he couldn't change Keturah's mind in this place, he'd make sure he'd change her parent's. It was the only way he was going to get her to come back with him willingly. She'd be obedient to what their wishes for her were.

***

Keturah grabbed her father's arm. "Please, don't speak with him, father. He'll want to force me to go back with him. And I don't want to." She plied him, her voice desperate. "He's an angry, violent man."

Her father shook his head. He shrugged her off. "Keturah, you can't leave him standing there. At some point, we have to greet him. He is your husband."

She went over and stood next to her mother by the low table in the room, watching the door furtively.

She could hear low voices in the courtyard, and then some chuckling and laughter. She gritted her teeth. What were they saying to each other? And why wasn't Joash tearing through the doorway in a fit of anger?

Her heart beat wildly, when he ducked under the solid stone arch, filling the space at the other side of the room. He stood there staring at her, his eyes gentle and caressing. Her father came in after him and gestured to the table. "Have a seat. You must be hungry. My daughter will bring you food."

Keturah almost groaned when Joash pulled out a spray of flowers and handed them to her. "Here." He gave a sidelong glance, smiling. "I picked these for you, before I came. I know how much you like them."

She looked at him as if she'd been stung. She couldn't believe he'd done such a thing. It wasn't at all like him. At once, she thought it must be some scheme of his to get her back. "What are you doing?" She spit out the words at him. She turned to her mother and father. "He's never given me flowers. He's not like this."

Her mother took her hand. "Keturah. Take them. He wants to make amends."

Keturah could have beat Joash over the head with his present at that very moment, seeing the way he was charming her mother with his handsome grin.

He held the flowers out again.

Keturah went to him and snatched them out of his hand, and tossed them in an untidy pile on the end of the table.

Joash's expression was one of amusement. He tipped his head courteously to her and smiled.

She stood against the wall, glaring at him.

Her mother took her arm. "Come, help with the food."

As they served both Joash and her father, Keturah eyed them suspiciously.

Joash told her father about the city of Bethel, and about the place he'd secured.

"Two hundred sheep?" Her father looked impressed. "And that many other livestock? You're a very well-set man for your age." He took a sip of his drink.

"The whole incident with our tribe was disheartening." Joash sounded as if he meant it.

Then, he looked over at Keturah. "But, when I brought Keturah back with me to be my wife, I knew things would be better."

Keturah's eyes could have been spears. She shot him an angry look that could've killed him.

He went on, ignoring her. "I've been fighting wars all my life and giving commands to my soldiers under me. But, I realized I never learned the art of how to treat a woman. But, I don't wish to lose Keturah, and want to try."

Her father had a serious expression on his face. Then, after some thought, he eyed Joash curiously and gave him a smile. He began to chuckle. "Well, when you find out, will you let me know?" And then with that, he let out a full laugh and held his stomach.

Keturah's mother went over to him and tapped his arm. "Now." She smiled. "If you'd like the rest of your meal, you'd best behave."

He pretended to be injured, but then he smiled to her and bowed. "For your food, I'll do anything you like."

Joash laughed at that.

Keturah let out a sound and took off the apron she was wearing over her tunic and threw it on a pile of mats against a sidewall. She stormed into the one room on the other side of the wall. She'd had enough of listening to them banter. She let out a breath and then put her hand to her stomach resting it there.

She couldn't believe what was happening with her parents and Joash. He was actually acting civil and not his usual demanding self, and her parents were buying it. Her mother seemed to be looking at him with stars in her eyes.

They were speaking of her love for Shiloh and how she'd been overtaken with homesickness.

Keturah scowled. She'd been so sure he was going to come crashing into the home demanding her return and was shocked when he didn't.

He must have had a lot of time to think about things on the ride over. He was surely presenting a very different side of himself. She worried what the outcome would be.

A while later, there was laughter and low voices beyond the courtyard, and she thought she could hear Caleb and Asher. She went back out through the dining area and into the courtyard, following the sounds. When she looked out across the field, she was shocked. Joash was with her brothers, showing them his sling and how to use it.

Them too? Her heart began to pump hard, and she quickly made her way to them, her face flaming. "What are you doing? Caleb? Asher?"

They turned, and when they realized she was there, they immediately looked guilty. "Joash was showing us his sling." Caleb smiled widely. "He's very good at it."

Asher piped in. "One of the famous left-handers." There was no denying the excitement and adoration in his voice.

Joash eyed Keturah with an interested look. He turned to her brothers. "I need to talk with Keturah. I'll show you another time."

They both looked disappointed, and then noticed their sister staring at them with angst. Caleb tugged on his brother's arm. "He'll show us, tomorrow. The caravan doesn't leave until the next day."

Asher dropped his head. "We'll wait." And then he turned to Keturah. "I still don't understand why you don't like him."

Her brothers both walked back to the house, Caleb turning back only once.

Keturah went to Joash and put her hand on his arm in a pleading gesture. "Why are you doing this?"

In his eyes there was a different look, one she'd never seen before. She couldn't read his thoughts.

He pulled her closer and lowered his head to hers, kissing her lightly on the lips and then more demanding. And then he put her away from him, leaving her breathless. "Because you're my wife. We belong together." And he turned and walked away to the house.

Keturah put her fingers to her lips, and a tear slipped down her cheek. She sat down on the ground and wrapped her arms around her knees, rocking gently back and forth.

For some reason, she knew, he'd get his way again. And there'd be nothing she could do to stop it.

*****

"Behold the Lord will carry thee away with a mighty captivity, and will surely cover thee." Isaiah 22:17 King James's Version

Chapter 34

Joash lifted Keturah onto the front of a cart, after she hugged each of her family members. Then he got up next to her and nodded to her mother and father and brothers.

They left town with the caravan. At least this ride would be easier. Joash had purchased a cart before he left, to carry their provisions, and for her to ride in. They planned to stop more frequently and rest with the others in the group.

Keturah watched Shiloh grow steadily smaller each time she turned around. She was empty and defeated inside, knowing there'd never be a home there to go back to. Her parents so much as said she wouldn't have a place if she decided to stay, and that she needed to go back with her husband and work out whatever differences they had.

Joash won.

He leaned down and whispered in her ear. "It'll be different. You'll see."

She closed her eyes and let out a breath. They had a long day of travel ahead of them.

***

Later at dusk, Joash set up the tent with the others. She eyed him curiously, while she sat beside him on a mat. All the women in the camp worked alongside him.

He stopped for a moment and went to her. He handed her a shawl. "Here."

She took it and wrapped it around her.

As much as he seemed to be trying to make amends, she still didn't trust that after the baby was born, this would all end. Right now, his concern was for the baby.

She got up to take a walk and look around the camp while she waited for him to finish with his work. But, before she could say anything to him, he immediately took a place by her side.

She made a face. "There's no need for you to come." She gave him a scathing look and hoped he'd take the hint.

But, instead, there was something in his eyes that glittered dangerously. He grabbed her arm and pulled her back. "It's not good to walk alone here."

His threats did nothing to frighten her, and she shook him off. "I'll be fine." She started to walk away from him.

He let out an exasperated sound. Then he spoke in a gentler tone, taking her hand. "The traders aren't safe. And they don't care if you're my wife."

She kept walking, but he didn't let go and stayed beside her. "I only needed to stretch my legs."

He was silent.

She walked past long row of tents and camels staked along the narrow path. The smell of campfires was strong, along with goat hair from the clothing and tents. There was a cool enough breeze, but dampness in the air made her feel tired.

She looked at the edge of the path where a campfire burned.

A chill went through her when she noticed a heavily bearded man, sitting beneath his tent on the side of the trail. His tooth was missing and he smelled of filth and dirt. There was something inherently evil in his face. His eyes were intense and dark, raking over her, sending a deep shudder through her. Even with Joash next to her, she didn't feel completely safe.

She put her shawl over her head and wrapped it tightly around her. The man was comparable to Joash in size. He made a low sound like a growl, as she walked past.

Maybe her husband was right. She wished she'd never seen that man. His twisted face kept stirring inside her.

She tugged on Joash's arm. "Let's go."

He eyed her curiously, then noticed the man on the path. "It's what I meant. There is safety in numbers."

She looked into his tender eyes, confused by what she saw there. Was he truly changing? It was difficult to believe.

Her pounding heart quieted by the time he deposited her back on the mat next to him, leaving her to watch him work. He didn't look at her until he was finished and then put out his hand. "We've a long day tomorrow. Get the rest you need."

A New Dance

She got up and went to him. The lids of her eyes felt heavy and her body weak from riding on the trail all day. She was tired and looked forward to a welcome sleep.

*****

"My beloved is unto me as a cluster of campfire in the vineyards of Engedi." Song of Solomon 1:14 King James's Version

Chapter 35

Joash scanned the hills in the distance as dusk approached. He'd have to get back to the caravan soon. He found a trustworthy family to leave Keturah with, so he could water his animals in the spring nearby and fill containers for the trip home. They'd have enough now to last until they arrived back at Bethel.

At least after she met up with that old trader in the caravan, she took Joash's advice to not wander off alone in the camp.

He thought of the last time he was with her. Lately, he realized not only he was changing, but Keturah was also. She never trusted him fully. But, since she left Bethel, it seemed any headway he had made, was lost. Something kept her at an arm's length from him, and he didn't know what it was. He wished he understood and would be able make things right between them.

He bowed his head and prayed, "Lord, show me the things I don't understand. Help me to gain her trust, so she can forgive me for what I've done in the past. Help me to love her the way she deserves to be loved. Help me to know how."

He lifted his head, and got up, eying the soft light of the caravan fires below the rocky hill. He climbed onto his horse and pulled the camel's rope from behind and started back to the others.

***

Keturah watched the horizon for Joash to appear, feeling a mixture of both apprehension and hope for his return.

She didn't want to travel the rest of the way to Bethel alone. Yet, there was also trepidation in her heart for what he made her feel, and she didn't want to be alone with him, either.

Keturah felt a hand go around her waist from behind. The only thing she could think of was that trader with the cold, dark eyes that swept over her in such a calculating way. Her heart pounded in her chest, and she struggled to break free.

A New Dance

"Whoa…it's me." It was Joash's low voice. "I was going to surprise you."

Relief flooded through her, when she realized who it was. She turned and practically flew into his arms, as he closed them around her.

She spoke to him through clenched teeth. "I thought you were the trader."

He laughed. "I smelled that bad?"

She shoved at him, unable to break free.

He smiled, amused. Joash leaned down and pressed his face in her hair. "I found a place to get the animals water." He laughed to himself. "Now, let's get ready to be on our way."

She sighed glad the journey was at an end. A short distance and they would be there.

*****

"Lo, children are the heritage of the Lord: and the fruit of the womb is his reward." Psalm 127:3 King James's Version

Chapter 36

Joash stood next to the gate of his home with Keturah at his side. He told his mother. "She needs rest. She's with child."

Mary ran over to Keturah and threw her arms around her. "A baby?" She smiled widely. "Oh!"

Then, she scowled at Joash and smacked him in the arm. "You shouldn't take a woman in this way across the country."

Joash lifted the swatch of fabric higher on Keturah's shoulder and smiled. "I was careful, mother, and let her rest along the way."

Mary shook her head. "You better have." Then she started hugging and kissing Keturah again. "A baby! My!"

Nissa giggled and took her turn hugging Keturah, until Joash pulled her away from them both. "I said rest. Not to smother her. She needs a bath and a bed to lie down on."

Keturah shook her head. "I'm fine. But can't wait to be clean again and get some sleep."

Both women led her into the home, chattering excitedly as they stepped through the doorway.

Joash called to his father. "Come, while I tie up Betsalel." And they both made their way to the rock hewn stable near the home.

***

"If she is with child, she needs rest and care."

Joash took the rope from his horse's neck and hung it over the gate of the stable. He sat on a large flat rock. "I treated her well. I'm trying to make changes, but it's not something that comes easy."

His father took a seat next to him. "None of it is, and some things are near impossible for us. But, with the Lord, he'll help. Just trust him."

Joash nodded. "I am doing better. But, you're right. The Lord still has much work to do."

***

Keturah sat down in the courtyard and began weaving some of the wool she and Nissa had spun, into a colorful piece of fabric. She looked into the fields and watched Joash from where she sat.

Her first thoughts had been that his change in behavior was only a ruse, to convince her family to let her go, but now she was beginning to wonder.

Just the other day, he'd brought her a meal and then cleaned up afterward, while she'd stared at him in shocked silence. Nissa had whispered in her ear, "He's different."

As much as Keturah wanted to believe it, she was still wary. He wanted a child, and she guessed he wanted to make sure there were no complications with the birth.

He stood from where he'd been placing seeds in the ground and looked her way. He seemed as if he wanted to stop what he was doing and go to her, but stooped over again and went back to what he was doing.

Keturah stared at him with a puzzled expression and then began to weave.

*****

"Let him kiss me with the kisses of his mouth: for thy love is better than wine." Song of Solomon 1:2 King James's Version

Chapter 37

On Sabbath, the family walked back to their home for a meal. All the preparations had been made the day before, so they sat down to eat loaves of bread, lentils and dried figs and drink some wine made from the vineyards.

"Here, Keturah," Nissa broke off some bread and handed it to her. "Take some lentils, too."

Keturah took a piece of bread and prayed and then began to eat. When she turned, Joash was studying her, his dark green eyes intense. Sometimes, he made her feel as if he could see into her very soul, and she felt exposed by the way he looked at her, especially in front of his family.

She quickly lowered her head, her cheeks warm, at the stirring sensation inside of her. He was the most handsome man she'd ever known, and it was so difficult for her to keep from showing the undeniable physical attraction she had for him. It bothered her that he seemed to know it, too.

Nissa shook her head. "Leave her alone, Joash. She's trying to eat." She poured him some wine and set the cup in front of him.

His father agreed. "Nissa's right. You're making her blush. Let her eat."

Joash took a swig of wine. And when his mother gave him a stern look, he let out a grunt and began to laugh. "All right. But, I don't understand why a man can't even look at his wife if he wants."

Keturah met his eyes again, this time with more courage and pushed a long braid behind her. "It'd be good to be able to keep focused on what's right on the Sabbath. We need to keep our thoughts on the Lord, today."

The others at the table nodded in agreement, with wide grins.

"Well said, Keturah." Simeon smiled. "A good daughter-in-law, she is."

Joash bit off a piece of his bread and chewed unceremoniously, smiling at her. "Fine. Eat your meal. But, later, we'll have time away from all your protectors."

A New Dance

She didn't quite know what he meant by his last comment, but at least for now, she might be able to eat without his constant attention.

The Sabbath was refreshing, and meals with Joash's family always felt special on this day of the week. They spent so much of each day working, there was little left for a restful talk. Keturah welcomed their light chatter and warm thoughts.

The food always seemed to taste better to her on Sabbath, also. Maybe because they didn't have to prepare anything that day and could just sit down and enjoy it. It always gave her a free feeling, one where she could take time to just pray and think of the Lord.

After the meal, Keturah helped put away any of the leftover food and then went to the doorway, looking out.

Joash came to her and took her hand. "Come with me."

She hesitated a moment, and then let him lead her out of the courtyard. "Let's bring Nissa."

He leaned down, brushing the top of her hair with his lips. "No. You don't need Nissa. I want to show you something."

He led her down a trail near the house that went up to a slightly wooded area in the valley near a creek. They stepped into the tree line. Branches were overhead, and it was dark under the canopy of the leaves. They went further down the trail.

"Where are we going?"

"Don't worry. We'll be there, soon enough. It's not far. It's something I discovered as a child."

As the rocky path deepened, Keturah quickened her pace and moved ahead. "We're getting closer?" She tugged on his arm.

Joash put his hand around her waist and slowed down. "See up ahead?"

She nodded.

He pointed. "There." The expression on his face was eager, as if he were holding onto a huge secret.

He took her to the edge of the rock formation. "Now, close your eyes. And I'll tell you when to open them."

She knit her brows and pinched the cloth of her tunic.

He smiled. "If you don't, I won't show you."

She took a step back at first, wary of his eagerness.

He laughed, as if he were entertained. "Keturah, I don't expect you to be like one of my soldier friends. Please, put your trust in me, just this once. I'm not ordering you, just asking."

He seemed sincere enough, so she gave a nod. She closed her eyes, relying on him to lead her.

She made her way over uneven rocky ground, as he led her up a slight incline and then, eventually onto solid footing. The sunshine streamed down on her from where they stood, and she listened to the sound of trickling water.

The air smelled fresh and clean and birds sang above their heads. She waited until he came to a stop.

He squeezed her hand. "Now. You can open them."

Keturah was sure it was going to be a waterfall.

When she looked up and opened her eyes, what was in front of her made her take a breath. She was, startled by the beauty of it.

"Oh." She uttered it softly, her voice a whisper.

He put his arm around her shoulders and held her against him.

A small stream of water flowed over rocks, higher than where they stood, moving gently down over the edge and past her feet. The trickling waterfall above them was a lovely sight. But, what took her breath away, were glittering rocks in the stream intermixed with the others, many of them shining in the sunlight like tiny jewels. The bed of the stream was dotted with them. They were like stars in the universe. Her mouth drew open, and she looked up at him in wonder.

"I haven't seen anything like this."

He bent down and took a sparkling stone out of the stream and handed it to her.

She held it up to the light and turned it in her hand, marveling at the way the sun's rays caught the surface and made it shine like a diamond. She closed her hand over it and held it to her, looking back over the riverbed. She felt as if she could stay in this place forever.

"It's the Lord's handiwork," she breathed. She didn't say anything for a long time, and then spoke quietly. "It's beautiful."

Joash turned her to him and gently lifted her face to his, meeting her eyes tenderly. "*You're* the Lord's handiwork. And my child's growing within you."

Tears formed in her eyes as he leaned down to kiss her. She knew her heart was changing toward him, and that there was nothing she could do to stop it. She ached inside at the thought that one day, after her child was born, she might not be so valuable to him.

A New Dance

She kept the stone he'd given her in her hand as they walked back together, pondering the changes between them and the ones she saw in Joash.

When they got back, she took her treasure to her room and lifted it up, turning it over in her hand. Out of the sunlight, there was only an occasional sparkle of light as a reminder of its beauty.

She sighed, praying their relationship would grow to be like the stones in the riverbed, into something lasting and real.

But, it'd be a time before she'd know it wasn't only a fleeting dream. She needed to know what Joash's feelings would be after their baby was born. She didn't want to let down her guard, just yet. A few more months and time would tell.

She rested her hand on her abdomen. She felt the thickening around her middle, even though she still wasn't showing to others. She smiled at the wonder of it. Regardless of her feelings toward Joash, she'd love the child with her whole heart and nothing could take that from her.

***

Joash patted his horse and looked back toward the house. Even though he sensed a change in Keturah, it wasn't as he wanted it to be. Despite the difference in him, she wasn't fully giving herself to him. He wished he knew how he could change that.

His father had been wise in regards to the whole matter. He should've consulted the Lord, before he went into her village and took her from all the things she loved. He'd gone his own way and was paying for it now.

And, through everything that had happened, he'd come to understand so much more about the consequences of sin. The wounds of it always ran deep, and though it sometimes felt like the easiest path, it never was a good one to take. It was best to follow the Lord's path, instead.

He remembered the look on Keturah's face when she opened her eyes to the shimmering creek. It gave him hope. Maybe there'd be redemption yet for him.

He got up on Betsalel and dug his heels into her side. "Ha!" He moved over the dusty path that led into the valley below. Maybe a ride on his devoted mare would do him good, time for prayer and meditation, trusting the Lord to handle the rest.

*****

"For the Lord hath called thee as a woman forsaken, and grieved in spirit, a wife of youth, when thou wast refused, saith thy God." Isaiah 54:6 King James's Version

Chapter 38

The following Sabbath, Keturah walked to Tirzah's home after she knew Joash was gone again, most likely out for a ride.

She pushed open the door and leaned inside. "Tirzah!"

Her friend came running up to her and threw her arms around her. Tirzah bubbled with excitement. "It's so good to see you! You must hear my news!" Her face was flushed, and it seemed as if she were holding back the most important discovery. "Come in and find out what's happened!"

Keturah smiled and locked arms with her friend, as Tirzah led her to a woven mat by a table.

"Let me get you some food and drink first."

"No. Food's not necessary right now. Let's not waste time with it."

Tirzah smiled. "We've been so busy lately, there's been no chance to get together. I'm glad you came. And that it's Sabbath, as we'll be able to rest."

Keturah nodded. "Yes." And then she took Tirzah's arm. "Now, tell me. What's happened?"

Tirzah wrapped her scarf tighter around her shoulders. "Isaac and I are going to have a child, too! I am so happy, I could almost burst."

Keturah let out a delighted sound and threw her arms around her friend. "Tirzah! Our babies will be close in age! They'll be friends!" She laughed. "I'm so excited!"

Tirzah nodded. "Yes, Isaac's very happy."

"Joash, too." And then, she sighed. "At least for that, he is."

Tirzah frowned. "Is he good to you, Keturah? What I mean is, he didn't seem like Hiram, and I know that's what you wanted."

Keturah didn't really know how to explain Joash's behavior, or her thoughts, but she tried to help her friend to understand. "He's kind to me now. He's changed."

"Oh, Keturah. I knew things would be better, especially when he found out how special you were."

Keturah sighed. "Well..." She fidgeted with her hands and then played with the folds of her tunic. "We'll find out soon enough, if his care and concern for me right now, are only for the child's sake. He made it clear to me from the beginning that this was the reason he married me."

"He better not do anything to hurt you." Her fists clenched, and she looked like she was about the breath fire. "And if he does, I'll be speaking with him."

Keturah smiled. "I'll be all right. But, I guess only time will tell what his intentions are."

Tirzah sat back down and took Keturah's hands in her own. "Well, if he does anything you don't like, then come to me."

Keturah laughed. "I don't know what you can do. But, I'll let you know."

"I'll do plenty. You'll see."

Keturah laughed again.

They spent the better part of the afternoon discussing their plans for their babies and preparation for the new arrivals. Keturah was even more excited about it after talking to her friend.

When she got up to leave, she felt a slight pain. She let out a soft breath and made a sound.

"Are you going to be all right?" Tirzah took her hand and stood next to her.

Keturah nodded. The pain subsided and went away. "Yes, it must be something I ate."

She felt better, straightening and heading to the door.

As she was going out, Isaac blocked her way.

She looked up at him and smiled. "Oh Isaac. Tirzah told me your news. I'm so happy for you both!"

He grinned widely, looking at Tirzah, who was just inside the house. "We're blessed." He took her hand. "And I'm very glad."

Keturah bowed to him. "Well, I need to get back to my own home."

He nodded, letting go of her. "It was good to see you."

"And you, also." She turned to her friend. "Bye, Tirzah!"

Tirzah smiled.

A New Dance

Keturah left through the doorway and into the courtyard then took to the road. Isaac had gone into the home.

As she took to the path, she looked down the road. Joash was coming toward her.

He looked furious. She stopped in her tracks, putting her hand to her throat. She wondered whatever it was that could make him so angry. She stood there, as the color drained from her face. "What is it?" She put her arms out to protect their child, when she saw how upset he was.

He stormed up the path and took her arm, clenching his fist. She winced. "Joash?"

His eyes were dark and blazing. He loosened his hold, but didn't let go. He growled low. "What have you done with Isaac? And to your friend?"

There was a raw, sick feeling that stole over her, and she felt the blood draining from her face. "Isaac? I'm four months with child."

He looked as if he could kill her at that moment, but let go, backing away. He was shaking. "You don't look it. Go home, Keturah! Now!"

Keturah remembered she'd been holding Isaac's hand at the doorway when she left Tirzah's home. She imagined what it looked like. "Joash! Wait!"

"I said to go home! I'll take care of it."

When she stood there staring blankly at him, he yelled again. "Go!"

Keturah stumbled blindly down the path, wiping tears from her face. He'd assumed she'd been with Isaac. What would he do to Tirzah's husband? She was afraid to know.

***

Joash stormed into Tirzah's home. Why would Keturah do such a thing to him? He was beside himself with anger. All the feelings of the past were coming back to haunt him. There were so many emotions running through him, he was afraid of what he'd do when he found Isaac.

"Where is he?" He crashed into a wooden bucket near the wall and kicked it out of the way as he burst into the room. His eyes were dark and narrowed to slits.

He came upon Tirzah, wrapped in her husband's arms. They both stared at him, bewildered.

Joash was looking at them like he was ready to do battle. "Keturah was here. With him."

"With Isaac?" Tirzah stepped between the men.

Then, she gave him a cock-eyed look and shook her head. "You mean at the door?"

Joash clenched his fists, his mouth a grim line, and nodded.

She put up her hand. "She was offering congratulations to my husband." She shook her head at the disbelief in his eyes.

Joash looked confused for a moment, staring from Tirzah to Isaac. Then, the smoldering in him suddenly died, and his face turned pale. "They weren't alone?"

Tirzah shook her head emphatically. "I was here, and she had just learned that we were with child. Why would you think she'd do anything with anyone ever? She's not like that."

Joash let out a breath, looking ashamed. He shook his head, bewildered.

Tirzah and Isaac both relaxed, staring at him with understanding.

"It's all right, but maybe you need to go after Keturah."

Then, Joash suddenly looked panicked. He groaned. "The baby. I have to go."

They nodded, and he left them standing there, as he tore out the door and down the path.

***

It was the second time Keturah felt a pain in her side. This one stopped her in her tracks, and she sucked in a breath. She put her hand to her side, and then noticed a spot of blood on the ground beneath her.

"Oh!" She cried out, as she dropped to her knees. She felt sick and dizzy, and the pain wouldn't leave. She was close to the home, but couldn't get up. All she could do was lie down in the path and hope someone would find her.

"Keturah?" Joash was behind her.

He got down next to her, cradling her in his arms. "What's wrong? What're you doing?"

A New Dance

She let out a painful sound. "Oh, Joash, it hurts. The pain."
She whispered it in his ear.

He noticed the blood on the road. "What's happened?" He
groaned, raining curses upon himself for his earlier behavior. "Our
baby!" He lifted her gently in his arms and began carrying her back.

"I'm sorry, Joash." Her voice was a murmur. "So sorry."

He didn't say anything, carrying her the rest of the way.

When he got into the home, he brought Keturah into a back
room and laid her on a soft pallet. "Nissa! Mother! I need your help!"

She moaned, holding herself at the waist.

Joash's mother came to her, cooing softly, and laying a cool
compress to her head. "It's all right, Keturah. You'll be fine. You'll
see."

"Is she going to get better? Is the baby?"

"Joash." His mother took his arm. "You mustn't stay. It isn't
a good place for a man to be."

He paced the floor. Keturah looked over at him and saw the
anger in his face as he looked at her. He was blaming her, now?

Keturah watched him leave, a fuzzy feeling enveloping her. It
seemed as if everything was slowing down around her. Nissa was close
to her, whispering in her ear.

She reached for Joash's sister, but then couldn't see her
anymore. Something bad was happening, and the pain was great. She
was losing feeling and was slipping away.

***

Joash was beside himself, after what happened. He still
couldn't believe the baby was lost. Four months old. It couldn't survive
at so early a birth. Its young life was taken too soon, and he'd never
know what the baby would have grown up to be like.

He dropped his head in his hands, as tears poured down his
face. How did one get over such a thing?

He blamed himself for yelling at Keturah and scaring her with
his false accusations and ridiculous claims. Could he never learn? How
could he have done this?

When he had found her in the road, his heart had practically
stopped. She was his life now, and the child was part of her. What had
happened was incomprehensible.

He hadn't spoken to her, but wanted to see her when she woke. He wouldn't blame her if she never wanted to talk to him again. He felt a shame for what he did and was angry for the temper he couldn't control.

And of all times, he'd been given orders from the military to report in the next town. There were skirmishes and they needed help with the fighting. He didn't want to leave Keturah, but didn't have a choice. He'd be able to wait one more day, to make sure her health wasn't jeopardized, but he'd have to go after that.

**

When Keturah woke a couple days later, Mary eyed her, concerned.

Keturah choked back a sob, remembering all that happened. "I lost the child, didn't I?" Her voice cracked.

Mary nodded her head, her face tearstained. "Oh my poor dear."

Keturah set to weeping, remembering bits and pieces of what happened. She recalled the horrible pain that gripped her in waves, tearing at her insides. Nissa had held her close and whispered that she'd be all right.

But now, a hollow empty feeling encompassed her, one even she couldn't explain or comprehend. The ache that she'd lost the baby was so deep, she wondered if she'd live through it. She didn't know such grief was possible. She'd carried the little one four months.

She rolled over on her side, a heartbroken cry escaping her lips. She thought of all the plans she'd made and how excited she'd been to see the baby.

She'd never know this little one and realized the child would never play with Tirzah's son or daughter. Her dreams of motherhood died inside her, and she felt as if she'd never recover.

And then she remembered Joash. She pulled the covering around her, recalling him in the room pacing, his face hard as stone. He had looked like a bull, as if he were waiting for the right time to smash everything in its path.

"Where is he?" She turned to Mary.

Mary didn't look up. "He got called away. But waited, to make sure you'd be all right."

176

A New Dance

Keturah stifled back another sob. She put her hands to her chest. So, she was left to face this alone. She couldn't imagine if she'd ever get through it. She'd lost their child, and was sure in the end he blamed her for it.

But, what did it matter? Both their dreams died with this baby. And all hope for the future.

She thought she'd seen changes in him, but realized she'd been wrong. In the end, she was sure he was still the same man she'd dealt with in Shiloh, having taken her for the sake of an heir and nothing more, incapable the kind of love she had dreamed of.

She cradled herself, tears washing over her face, while her cries turned to muffled sobs. Her eyes darkened at the thought of his return. The thought of it sickened her. It was the last time she'd ever endure pain like this, and surely not for him.

Mary wrapped her arms around Keturah and held her tightly. "You're a strong girl. The ache will lessen with time. Grieve, now. But, remember that things will be better, someday."

Keturah curled deeper under the covers. She didn't know if what Mary told her were true, but held onto a tiny thread of hope that it was. But for now, she mourned the loss of her child. Her baby was gone.

*****

"If we hope for that we see not, then do we with patience wait for it?"
Romans 8:25 King James's Version

Chapter 39

Three months passed since the tragic day. Keturah woodenly went about her tasks, the hollow feeling still inside her, but she realized the pain had lessened and was not so intense. Maybe, things would get better over time, and she might someday experience even a sliver of her former self again. At least she was up now and helping again with the chores.

Nissa patted her arm, kissing her on the cheek. "Tomorrow's Sabbath. After dinner, we're going to Tirzah's home, and they've planned to play music there."

Keturah sighed, smiling. Maybe an outing would take her mind from things. "It sounds good, Nissa. I'm glad I'll be with you."

She pulled a loaf of bread from the opening of the stone oven in the courtyard and looked over the horizon. There was a lone rider coming in the distance.

Her heart wrenched inside. Joash was back. How could she face him, after losing their child?

Nissa noticed her brother at the same time. "Joash is back and safe. Finally!" She ran into the house. "Mother! He's home!"

Mary and Simeon came out to watch as he rode closer.

Keturah crossed her arms in front of her.

When he reached them, he got off his horse, his eyes immediately seeking her out. His face was difficult to read, as if he didn't quite know what he could expect from her.

He went to her and held her close. He didn't say anything, but after a time, finally let go and went to his other family members, greeting them in turn.

Keturah went back to the hearth, wrapping a piece of cloth around the loaf she'd pulled out. She bristled and hardened herself to the emotions that threatened to spill from her.

With the loss of their child, something dark had gripped her inside, and she felt as if whatever it was, it were tearing at her very soul. She'd never experienced anything remotely like it, and couldn't seem to let it go. Despair seemed to be her closest friend lately. And her darkest emotions seemed directed toward her husband.

Her eyes were like arrows aimed at Joash as she watched him tenderly embrace Nissa. She could think of nothing he could do that would induce her to respond to him in any way. She couldn't deal with the loss of another child and the guilt that accompanied it. Things wouldn't go back to the way they were before he left, and she was determined to make sure they didn't.

***

Joash wasn't expecting as cold of a greeting as he got from Keturah. He wasn't sure what to do to make her feel differently. She was obviously still caught up in her grief and would need time to heal.

He thought things might have changed for them while he was gone, especially with the loss of the child, but not as much as what they had. He'd never seen such bitterness on Keturah's face when she looked at him before, even after he'd taken her from Shiloh. It was difficult, as he wanted to share in the mourning with her and be a comfort to her. After seeing her, he realized that it would be near impossible, at least until she could find it in her heart to forgive and trust him again. He bowed his head and prayed. She obviously blamed him for the death of their child.

***

Nissa grabbed Keturah's hand and pulled her along. "Come! They're playing music, the lutes."

The trepidation in Keturah's heart seemed to grow, as she went through the gate and into the courtyard of Tirzah's home. She stepped cautiously around the corner and looked for her friend.

Immediately, her eyes rested on her Tirzah's growing waistline. Tirzah was about five months along with child, slightly more than she had been, when she'd lost her baby.

The emotional response to seeing her friend at this stage in her pregnancy tore at some old wounds, but it also seemed to open some new ones. Fear for Tirzah's newborn child, happiness for her friend, and pain over the loss of her own baby son, all struck her at the same time.

She gripped Nissa's hand tighter.

Then, she noticed Joash's movement from the corner of her eye. His face was a hard mask, as he bent his head to acknowledge Isaac and Tirzah, and then turn to study her. She could guess what he was thinking as he went to the outer wall of stone and looked out into the distance over the horizon.

When she approached Tirzah and Isaac, Keturah reached out and hugged her friend. "It's good to see you both."

Tirzah patted her arm gently. There was pain in her eyes. "I'm glad you're here." She didn't speak of the baby growing inside her and pulled her shawl over her waistline. "Go and take a seat on the mats, both of you." She tipped her head to Keturah and Nissa. "There's so much food. I don't know how everyone will eat it all."

Keturah squeezed her friend's hand and then let go.

Isaac nodded. "It's true. We're blessed in so many ways."

He eyed the wrap around Tirzah's waist then looked back at Keturah. "With the harvest." He was clearly uncomfortable, and then contrite. "I'm sorry, Keturah. I didn't mean..."

Keturah sighed. "It's all right, Isaac. I knew what you meant. I'm glad for your blessings on all accounts."

She took Nissa's arm, and they sat on the mat. When Joash came to the table to join them, Keturah tugged on Mary's tunic. "Sit here."

Mary took a place by her daughter in law. "Are you all right?"

"Yes." Keturah's eyes met Joash's. "It'll be good to talk."

Joash took a seat further away. He began loading his plate with meat, grapes, olives and pieces of bread, and then poured a full glass of wine.

Keturah sighed. Nothing seemed to quench his appetite. She watched him devour the food on his plate and take more.

She reached out and picked up a couple figs and gnawed on the edges. She didn't feel particularly hungry, but forced herself to eat something.

Simeon sat on the other side of the mats and filled his plate. He looked at Joash. "Will you be home for a while?"

Joash swallowed what he was eating and washed it down with some drink. "I hope. There's still a lot to do."

Simeon nodded. "With the wheat and vineyards and all those animals, we really should think of hiring some workers."

A New Dance

"I can get a lot of it done. But, if I have to leave, you might consider it."

Simeon shook his head. "Yes, I've kept this in mind."

Keturah half listened to the conversation around her, as the night grew longer, but didn't seem to be able to make sense of any of it. Her thoughts still wandered to the loss of their firstborn child.

There were too many reminders in this place. Tirzah, Isaac, Joash, the path to Tirzah's home, the heat of the day, and the new child growing in her friend's womb. It all seemed a bit too much, too soon. Sometimes it felt as if her heart was being ripped apart from the inside out.

She wished she were back at the house working. She used to love Sabbath. But now, it was like a burden to bear, with too much time to think. It was easier when her hands were busy. It seemed to keep her mind freer from the things she didn't want to think about.

Lately, there was also this feeling of guilt she harbored that seemed to stick in her like a knife. She felt bad she wasn't there for Tirzah, and it niggled at her insides. The thought never seemed to go away. In times like these, it was as if grief was becoming her newest ally, and a destructive one at that. And the Lord seemed far away.

She wanted her friend to be happy and hated ruining things with her own sullen moods and newfound temper. It should've been a time for rejoicing, not for sorrow. But, every time she was around Tirzah, Keturah felt she was weighing her friend down. And she didn't want to do that.

Keturah eyed the outer area of the home.

The lutes were playing and the people were laughing amidst the beat of drums. There was a heady scent of wine and food, mingling with incense.

She sat there trying to take it all in, but couldn't. The whole celebration seemed to run together in her mind in an endless stream, and life as she knew it, seemed to be flying past her at a pace she couldn't keep up with.

She got up, whispering to Nissa. "I'll be back."

Joash was deep in conversation with his father, while Mary listened to them. Nissa nodded, and then she turned back to her friend on the other side of her.

Keturah made her way across the courtyard and out of the gate. She stood on the hillside, staring at the late afternoon sky. Tears began to flood her eyes, and she began to weep. Her shoulders shook, as she knelt onto the ground, gulping back sobs.

"Keturah." A low voice whispered her name.

She turned.

She pushed the tears from her eyes and straightened. "What are you doing here?"

Joash was behind her. His brow was furrowed, and he had a pained expression on his face. "To see if you were all right."

"I'll be fine. Please. Go and leave me."

He placed his hands on her shoulders and turned her to him. "Are you sure?"

She didn't like the tender look in his eyes. She didn't want his sympathy. "I said to go!"

"Joash." Simeon came up behind his son. "I think it's probably best you don't stay. I'll take her home."

"But..." He looked agitated.

Keturah didn't look at him. "I want to be with your parents."

Joash shoulders tensed. He grit his teeth together, clearly at odds with them.

"Joash." His father put his hand on his arm. "She only needs time. Stay with Nissa. Give your sister a ride later."

"But, father."

Simeon nodded to him. "She'll be all right with us. We'll see to it."

Keturah sniffed and wiped her cheeks, turning from them. She wrapped her shawl tighter around her.

His sandals retreated behind her, and he was gone.

Good, she thought.

"Do you want to go now, Keturah?" Simeon came up behind her. "I'll get Mary."

She looked pained. "Oh. You don't have to do that."

Mary came to the gate. "Joash said to come out." She looked worried. "Is everything all right?"

Simeon put his hand on Keturah's shoulder. "She's tired is all. I'm going to take her home."

Mary spoke softly. "I need the rest, too. The three of us can go."

"Oh, Mary. Don't leave on my account."

Mary shook her hand. "No, no. Both Simeon and I want to help." She looked at her husband. "We'll wait until you bring the cart around."

Simeon nodded. "I'll be right back." He left quickly and disappeared around the corner to where the animals were tied.

Keturah apologized again. "I don't know what happened. I always think things are better, and then something happens, and it all starts again."

Mary took her hand. "Grief is like that, so don't worry. You've lost a child. It isn't an easy thing."

And then she added. "But, don't try to run from it, Keturah. It's necessary. You should experience the pain, as difficult as it is. You'll heal quicker."

Keturah lifted her hair over her shoulder and played with the ends. She didn't say anything, but nodded.

Mary took her shawl and wiped the tears from Keturah's face. "Time will lesson the pain, too."

Keturah looked at her warmly. "You're like my mother. I couldn't ask for more."

Mary smiled, but looked solemn. "I hope Bethel will someday feel like home to you."

Keturah nodded. "Thank you, Mary. You've been good to me."

Simeon rode around the corner of the courtyard and out to the road with the wagon. A couple of mules hitched to it, clomped down the hard path. Simeon stopped the wagon when he got to them, and they climbed in.

As they rode away, Keturah looked back at the house and noticed Joash standing by the gate, watching them.

She turned, drawing closer to Mary, not wishing to share any of this with him.

***

Joash went back inside and stood against an outer wall alone.

Tirzah went over to him. Her eyes were like hot coals. "What did you do?" she bit out. Her lips were pursed, and she looked as if she were on fire.

Joash didn't answer.

Kara S. McKenzie

"Well?" She scowled. "Where is she?"

Joash held out his hand. A gruff chuckle spewed from him, and he shrugged his shoulders and looked away as if defeated. "Do I have every woman in the territory mad at me? She went home. I tried to go with her, but she wouldn't have me."

Isaac came to stand beside his wife. "It's only that Keturah's grieving. Joash didn't do anything."

Tirzah looked down at her waistline and then back to Joash.

Joash's eyes moistened with tears. "We're both grieving." He looked away. "And I don't know what to do. I need her."

He fingered the sling at his side. "But, I suppose I belong elsewhere." And then he smiled solemnly. "I'm sure she'd rather have me die a thousand deaths on the battlefield, than be with her."

Tirzah stared at him, like she was seeing him for the first time. She looked contrite. "I'm sorry. I didn't think."

"It'll all be well in time. Things will get better. I'm sure." But, he wondered if they would.

"Is she with your father?"

He nodded. "Yes, she insisted on going home with them. I'm to bring Nissa back." He looked across the room to where his sister was sitting.

Isaac patted his shoulder. "It may be some time. I think that young man over there is interested in her."

Joash's eyes narrowed, as he noticed a dark-haired man laughing at something his sister said. She was looking down, but she had a smile on her face.

"Or sooner." His voice was a low growl. "Now that she's speaking, she needs to know when it's appropriate."

"Be easy on her, Joash. There's no harm done. He's not a bad sort."

Joash said a quick prayer so he wouldn't do anything impulsive that would get him into worse trouble. He nodded, taking a breath. "Thank you. And for listening."

He went to the table and took Nissa by the arm, gently lifting her to her feet. "Father and mother want us home."

And then he scowled at the man across the table and looked around. "And any man who wishes to speak with my sister, needs to talk to my father or I, first."

184

A New Dance

Nissa smiled sweetly and blushed. "My brother will see me home." She waved to the others around her.

She turned to leave with him after saying goodbye, and Joash led Nissa out the door.

***

Nissa grabbed the edge of the wagon to steady herself, when the cart hit a bump in the road. "Keturah left early?"

Joash's brows furrowed. "You knew she did." He flicked the reins. "And don't try to change the subject, Nissa. Who was that young man?"

Nissa looked up at her brother and smiled. "His name's Jesse. He lives near Tirzah with his family."

"And how do you know him?" Joash frowned. "What did you say?"

Nissa put her hand on his shoulder. "He's my friend's brother. And I told him I mustn't be speaking to him."

"But, he was laughing at what you said."

Nissa nodded. There was color in her cheeks. "Because I told him to talk to father."

Joash hands on the reins loosened their grip. He looked at her sidelong. "It's what you said?"

Her eyes were dancing. "Yes."

"And no more."

"No. Nothing."

And then he smiled, as if amused. "So, he'll be calling?"

Nissa sighed, smiling impishly. "Maybe. If my older brother didn't scare him away." And then she giggled. "I hope he'll visit."

Joash suddenly groaned, looking down at her. "I guess I can't seem to do a whole lot right lately."

"Lately?" Nissa laughed.

Joash stared out over the hills and sighed. "You're right. I don't think much before I act. I wish I were more like father." I have a lot to learn.

Nissa put her hand on his arm, and her eyes softened. "Oh, no, Joash. You're the way the Lord made you. And he saw what he made, and it was good."

"But, I've so many weaknesses?" His expression was solemn.

185

Nissa's eyes lit. "We all do. But, the Lord sees your heart. All those other things are meaningless to him, when he knows how you're trying. Even when you fail."

Joash eyed her curiously.

She smiled. "It's what our forefathers believed, that we must walk in faith. It's what the Lord would want."

Joash nodded. "I suppose this is good, then."

"It is." Then, Nissa took his arm, again. "How's Keturah?"

He shrugged. "She wouldn't speak to me." When their home came into view, he looked down the road. "But, I guess we'll know soon."

"Keep praying to the Lord for her, Joash. She's going through a hard time, and may not be seeing things clearly. He'll help her through this."

He sighed. "I just hope my prayers will be enough. My sin in going against the Lord and not consulting him was great. Maybe I'll have to keep paying for this."

Nissa shook her head. "I don't think so." Her eyes took on a glow. "You and Keturah have paid a high price for sin, but the Lord is merciful, and his mercy is higher than that. I'm sure he has something wonderful in store for you both, in his time."

Joash looked hopeful. Then he nudged his sister with his shoulder. "And you say this, even after all the things I've done to you?"

Nissa laughed and pushed him back. "Well, now that I think about it..."

"Don't. I liked what you said before." When they neared their home, he pulled on the reins, and the wagon slowed to a stop.

Nissa giggled. "It'll be good, brother. You'll see. The Lord can do a whole lot more than we know."

He gave her a sidelong glance and sighed. "I'm glad for that."

He helped her down from the wagon and sent her inside, while he stayed out to take care of the animals, and take Betsalel for a ride.

***

Joash watched the house from a distance from atop his horse. Keturah was working in the courtyard next to his mother.

She looked over at him and then quickly away, going back to her work.

186

A New Dance

His eyes narrowed. If she'd quit hiding behind his family members and let him get close enough to at least talk to her, they might have a chance. But, every time he tried to get near, she'd start an argument, and either Nissa or his mother or father would step in and tell him to let her be. How could anything ever get resolved this way?

He kicked his heels into the side of his horse and slapped the reins, and rode out into the countryside. Betsalel would enjoy a brisk run this afternoon. And he'd find a place to pray.

*****

"When I looked for good, then evil came unto me: and when I waited for light, there came darkness." Job 30:26 King James's Version

Chapter 40

Joash looked out over the mountaintop. He rubbed his hands together. The air was cool, and the evening was approaching.

He put his hands to his head. Why had his life taken such a turn? Where was the Lord? And where were the answer to his prayers? What was the Lord doing, and why hadn't he responded?

Keturah seemed more distant than she'd ever been, and she didn't seem to be showing any improvement. And he was more frustrated and agitated with her than ever.

He prayed for patience, and he had none. He prayed for peace, and it was definitely not there. He prayed for mercy, but he couldn't even forgive himself. And he prayed for reconciliation with Keturah, but she'd have none of it.

He wondered, when he finally trusted the Lord and prayed faithfully, why he felt so alone?

It was so difficult for him to hold back and wait for the Lord's timing. It wasn't in his nature.

But, what else could he do? Everything he tried, failed. He'd never felt so utterly dependent upon the Lord.

He remembered when he first started to pray, and it was as if the Lord's presence was right there with him. But, now there was nothing. And all he could do was wait and hold on to the faith he had, that the Lord was real, even when it didn't feel that way.

He looked up at the night sky, as the stars began to appear. The path to the Lord seemed broken. He wondered if this is how it felt when Moses waited for Pharaoh to release the Israelites, or for Joseph to wait to be released from prison.

Maybe, it was time to let Keturah go, and put her in the Lord's hands, to pray in faith and believe, so the Lord could do what he planned with her.

He lifted his hands in prayer. "She's yours. Have her, to your will."

He was sure it's what the Lord wanted, for him to have no other gods.

A New Dance

He bowed his head in prayer. "When the time's right, let me know, and I'll do as you wish. But, I'll wait now for you."

He felt as if his soul was being torn from him. It was if he were Abraham, laying his son, Isaac on the altar. He needed to have the same faith and trust. Whatever the outcome, for Keturah's sake, he knew it was the right thing to do.

*****

"Thy cheeks are comely with rows of jewels, thy neck with chains of gold." Song of Solomon 1:10 King James's Version

Chapter 41

Keturah noticed the light in Nissa's eyes, as a young man walked down the path toward the gate. He shook hands with Simeon and was welcomed into their courtyard. Simeon gestured for the man to go into the house with him.

As they walked past, Nissa lowered her head and concentrated on the wooden bowl in her hands, where she'd been cutting pieces of cheese for the meal.

Keturah was grinding roasted lentils to press into cakes for the dinner meal, curious as to why they had a visitor. "Who's that?"

Nissa smiled, her cheeks rosy. "My friend's brother, Jesse."

"What's he doing?"

Nissa didn't answer, but smiled, her head down.

When he came through the gate, he looked over at her and took off his head covering, pushing his hands through his hair. He smiled and tipped his head and then went into the house with Simeon. He was carrying a package in his other hand.

Keturah let out a knowing sound. "Oh. So, when did this happen?" Her expression brightened. "He's come for you?"

Nissa smoothed out her skirt and pulled her braid in front of her, playing with it. "Maybe." Her voice was barely a whisper. "I don't know."

Keturah thought back to a time in Shiloh. Nissa was lucky she'd be able to have a man her parents chose for her.

She reached out and touched Nissa's arm. "You like him?"

Nissa nodded. There was a light blush on her cheeks. "He's a good man. I'd be honored to have him as a husband."

Keturah nodded. "I'm happy for you."

Nissa leaned close to Keturah. Her eyes were solemn. "Joash would be a good husband, if you let him."

Keturah frowned. "Our marriage will never be that way. Too many things have happened for it to work for us."

"But, the Lord can change things. He can make things right."

A New Dance

It was true, Keturah thought. The Lord could do what he wanted.

But, for some reason, he hadn't come through for her and hadn't answered her prayers. "He can. But, the question I have, is will he?"

Nissa placed the squares of cheese on a flat basket and wrapped them with cloth. She set the tray on the steps beside her. "Oh, I believe so, Keturah. The Lord's so good. I know it can't be easy for you to believe this after all you've been through, but don't give up on his love for you. Don't let it turn you bitter."

Keturah placed the lentil cakes in the stove with a tool and sat in front of them, watching them bake. She didn't answer, not knowing what to say.

Not long after, Simeon came to the doorway. "Nissa. I've something to ask you."

Nissa got up, wiping her hands on her tunic and then brushing it off. She pushed her braid behind her and straightened her hair, smiling at Keturah.

"Yes, father." She followed him into the house and disappeared behind closed doors.

Keturah flipped the lentil cakes, which were sizzling and browned. She put the finished ones on a clay platter.

She lifted her eyes to the doorway and felt a hard lump inside her throat and swallowed it, pushing back the tears filling her eyes. She wished Nissa would be as happy as she might've been one day.

She lifted a cloth over the lentil cakes and let them cool next to the other food to take in later, when matters in the house were finished being discussed.

*****

191

"He will not suffer me to take thy breath, but filleth me with bitterness."
Job 9:18 King James's Version

Chapter 42

"Father gave his blessing." Nissa's smile was wide and her eyes bright. She leaned close to Keturah and grabbed her hand. "I'll be moving in with Jesse's family as his wife soon."

Keturah gave Nissa a hug. "I'm so glad for you. I think Jesse will make a good husband." Her eyes were warm.

She looked across the room. Joash was staring at her with narrowed eyes. She lifted her chin, her gaze stony. "I'm glad you'll have a traditional marriage."

Nissa nodded, her face radiant. Then, she looked up from the embroidery she was working on and noticed Keturah's expression, and her eyes dimmed. "But, we have to accept what the Lord gives us." She eyed her brother with a forlorn expression.

Keturah set her needlework down and stood up. "Yes, but, sometimes it's not so easy."

Then she patted Nissa's shoulder. "Come now. It's a special time. Don't let me ruin any of it for you. The Lord will be with you and Jesse. He'll bless your marriage." Her look was tender.

She turned to the doorway. "Now, I need to go and take care of those chickens. They haven't had their meal."

She took a sack of seed and slung it over her shoulder.

Nissa smiled. "Don't let the little rooster get the better of you, sister."

Keturah shook her head. "He doesn't frighten me. I've dealt with much worse than him." She wouldn't look at her husband, but could feel his dark stare from across the room.

She ducked under the doorway, welcoming the sunshine and brightness of the day.

***

Keturah sprinkled seed outside the courtyard in an area away from the entrance where the chickens were poking at the ground. They came to her clucking and squawking, as soon as they realized she was scattering food for them.

The young rooster Nissa spoke of, was crowing the loudest, but had learned not to tangle with her and kept his distance. She made sure there was enough for all of them for the evening, and then laid the sack of feed on the top of the courtyard wall.

She leaned down to pet a little black goat that came running up to her. "You look like my Betsalel." She murmured it softly in his ear. She began to pull some burrs from his fur.

She didn't realize Joash had come out of the house and was standing behind her until he spoke to her, his voice low. "As if you're the only one suffering."

Keturah stood up.

Every fiber in her being, wanted to injure him, to the point where he would leave her alone, forever. "Ha! You?" Tears welled up in her eyes. "I've made you suffer?"

Joash stalked over to her, grabbing her arm and pulling her to him. "Stop. You don't know what you're saying." His face looked pained.

Keturah drew in a breath. Joash was leaving her alone, and she hadn't had to deal with his closeness to her. But now, a warm sensation ran through her, and she ached for his touch.

She lowered her lashes and didn't look at him. Why did she have to be so weak? He wanted an heir, and he would make it happen, regardless of her feelings.

His mouth lowered to hers.

Tears fell down her cheeks. He didn't love her, and she'd be giving herself to him without regard to it. There should've been more to their marriage than this. Nothing seemed right.

She looked up at him again through tear-filled eyes, and his expression suddenly changed. He let go of her and backed away. There was a look of despair in his expression, mixed with anger.

He didn't speak, but turned and went to the stable and left her standing there, confused and alone. What did he want? Why did he leave?

He came out with his horse and got on without looking her way, turning toward the wide field beyond their home, and rode away. He quickly disappeared beyond her sight into the distant rocky hills.

She shook her head, bewildered. Something was wrong. What was he waiting for? What was she to do?

*****

"A time to weep, and a time to laugh; a time to mourn, and a time to dance;" Ecclesiastes 3:4 King James's Version

Chapter 43

Keturah stared at the horizon in the direction of Shiloh. How had her life taken such turns, when she was faithful to the Lord and tried so hard to follow him? Why had he given her such troubles?

She guessed it was only a matter of time, before the ruse Joash had been playing would end and things would change. The cracks were beginning to show through the armor he'd built around himself, and he couldn't fool her with his kind looks and careful manner. There was a fire that was brewing down deep inside him. When would he have had enough, and his patience with her end?

He was on his way back from a ride and tied his horse to a tree nearby. The expression on his face was determined, as he made his way to her. She guessed this was the day things would come to that.

"You're leaving with me, now, Keturah."

She put up a hand. "No." Her heart began to pound. He was taking long strides toward her.

Simeon came out into the courtyard, taking a place by Keturah's side. He moved closer to her. He looked at his son. "Leave her be, Joash. We've discussed this. She needs time."

Joash stormed over to them, taking Keturah by the arm. "I know what I'm doing. There's a time for everything. And I'm done waiting." He started dragging her across the courtyard behind him toward the gate.

Keturah tried to right herself, but kept tripping as he pulled her along. "I told you to stop!" She hissed it through her teeth. "Let go of me!"

Nissa and Mary came running outside. "Do something."

Mary looked at Simeon. "He's going to hurt her!"

Simeon knew he was no match for his son, but he followed him to the gate. "Son, let's talk, instead." He watched as Joash lifted Keturah up on the backside of the horse and got up behind her.

"No." Joash shook his head. "She's coming with me."

Keturah felt Joash's arm grip her around her waist. She knew it was useless to try to push him away, as he dug his heels into the horse, and slapped the reigns on the horse's backside. She turned, eying his hard jawline. She realized he wasn't going to do things her way anymore.

She guessed it would come to this eventually, but knew Joash would no longer have the upper hand.

She shrugged, feeling dead inside to what used to induce her to try with him. All the physical strength and fury he posed didn't frighten her anymore, and it would do nothing for him this time, to sway her thoughts.

She realized how much she had changed, after facing the difficulties she had in the past year. Little seemed to affect her, like it used to. She figured her life was the Lord's will, and he'd do with her what he would. And right now, she wanted nothing more than to be free from her wounded. Joash held no power over her, like he had before. She wasn't afraid of him, either.

They flew down the path that led out of town and into the wilderness. They rode for miles along a barren stretch, until they came to a rocky hillside. The top of it was covered in tall shrubs, and it rose high over the countryside. He reigned in his horse, and they began to climb, weaving over rocky ground and some green shrubs, until they reached a tent set up in the middle of it high at the top. A bubbling spring was trickling down the side of the mountain, next to a fire that had almost died out.

Keturah gave him a quelling look as he got off and lifted her down, setting her next to him on the ground.

She looked at the tent, and her expression hardened. "Why are we here? What do you think to gain from it?"

Joash let go of her and tied the horse's rope to a shrub. He sat down next to the fire. His expression was unreadable.

Her eyes were hard, and her mouth was set in a firm line.

He looked up at her with an indifferent expression. "We need to talk...without interference from my family."

She turned her back on him, pushing angry tears from her eyes. "But, I've nothing to say to you."

Joash didn't answer. She could hear him lying sticks on the fire and stoking the flames.

She sat down a distance from him, wrapping her arms around her legs and staring blankly over the horizon. The sun had gone down, and it was growing dark around them. She shivered from the chilly night air.

"Come, Keturah. You'll be cold there. Move closer."

She didn't budge. "I don't want to, and don't care if I freeze." It was cold and she would have liked to sit closer to the fire, yet, she also wanted to suffer and hurt Joash in the process, and make him feel as if he were the cause of it. Then he'd take her home.

He sighed. "Please. I'll bring you back tomorrow night, if you come near the fire."

She inched toward the flames, but kept to the far side of it, away from him. She could stand one day.

He let out a breath. "What can I do? Tell me what will make things right between us?"

She just sat there staring at the crackling fire, not really knowing how to answer. She couldn't say. She grabbed a blanket next to her and wrapped it around her, hugging it tightly to her body and curled up on her side.

She only had to endure this night and one day with him, and he'd take her back. She'd wait for the time to pass. Then he might leave her in peace.

As she began to drift off, she heard him taking steps toward her. He gently lifted her up, carrying her to the tent and in through the doorway. She pretended to sleep.

He put her down and leaned over and kissed the side of her face. She tensed at his touch, pulling her wrap tighter around her.

It surprised her when he got up and went back out to the fire.

She rolled over, looking out of the tent to where he sat quietly staring off in the distance. What was it he wanted, her to go to him? Why did he bring her here?

She closed her eyes, angered by the thought. Then, she turned back over. It would be a long night. She was having none of it. Not anymore.

***

Joash began to pace outside the tent, turning his gaze to the stars overhead. He promised Keturah he'd take her home after one day. Why did he give her his word and tell her this?

What could he say to change her mind? Would the time be too short?

He had to get ahold of himself, to trust. He bowed his head and said a quick prayer.

He'd been praying, and thought he clearly had heard what he needed to do. But now, Keturah wouldn't even speak to him. How could he reach her in one day? They were no closer now, than they'd been the day he first saw her. Their relationship seemed never to get past the sins of Shiloh. Was he supposed to bear those consequences for the rest of his life?

And yet, why would the Lord instruct him to bring her to this place, if nothing was to happen? There had to be a reason.

He calmed at the thought.

Their marriage may have been wrong from the beginning because of his hand and willfulness, but it was the Lord's marriage now, and Joash had to believe in the Lord's abilities.

And regardless of Keturah's feelings for him and how difficult it might be, he had to have faith in the Lord for all things.

***

The next day felt like one of the longest days of Keturah's life. She sighed, as she stared at the fire next to her. She'd agreed to stay for the full time, and now it was finally drawing to a close. She breathed a sigh of relief, knowing Joash wouldn't go back on his word.

She ached to go back to the mindless tasks at the estate, as it was easy to avoid him there in her busyness. They'd been in this place too long.

He stirred the fire. "You told me you'd stay, but haven't said a word since morning. How can anything good come from that?"

She felt as if she might burst, if she held her feelings in any longer. There'd been a churning feeling growing inside her all day. "Good? Do you think anything we've had together has been good?"

Joash let out an exasperated breath. "I don't know anymore."

Her face flamed. "When you took me from Shiloh, you told me you what you wanted, and I've not forgotten it." She moved away from him and choked back a sob. "But, you can take a concubine for that."

Joash took her by the shoulders, shaking his head. "I don't want a concubine or any other wife."

"But, why? With one of them, you could have your wish. You wouldn't have to deal with me."

Joash suddenly looked lost and as if he didn't know what to say. He wrung his hands together and turned to her with deep frustration in his eyes. He looked like a broken man, not like the one Keturah knew.

She watched him closely, wondering at the changes she'd seen. She felt a tinge of guilt run through her, seeing his defeated look. He'd always been so self-assured and confident. He didn't seem quite the same person.

He spoke quietly. "I'm sorry, Keturah. And I really do mean this."

She bristled at his words. "For bringing me here?" She shrugged. "It's of no consequence. We'll be leaving soon, and I can go back to my work."

"No, Not for bringing you here." He groaned. "For everything." He almost choked on his words.

Keturah took a step back. She shivered from the chilly night air and the light wind beginning to churn. "What are you talking about?" She rubbed her shoulders.

Joash reached for her, but she drew back. He stopped and shoved his hand through his hair, impatiently. "I thought you knew I changed and that I wanted to be different. I know you might not believe it, but I've felt bad for everything I've done. I know it was wrong to take you from your family and home for the purposes I did, and I shouldn't have done it. I've paid dearly for not listening to my father."

Keturah drew in a breath. "You're saying this, because you want me to come to you."

He patted the side of his horse. "I want you back with me. But, not for the reasons you think. You don't understand."

He looked at the ground and then at her, again. His eyes were moist. "I've tried to become the man you wanted me to be. And I thought you knew that the changes I've made have been for you, but I see that you didn't understand it."

He looked up at the stars that were coming out. "I've been praying for the Lord to help us, and I don't understand why he's silent. I love you Keturah, and I'd do anything to know that you loved me back. I've done so much wrong and have hurt you so badly. I wish I could go back and do things all over again, the right way."

Keturah turned to him, confused. Her mouth drew open as she eyed his solemn expression, and it was as if she were suddenly seeing him for the first time. She stared at him, lifting her hand to her chest and holding it there. "You said, you were praying?"

He nodded. "I've been speaking to the Lord everyday for a long time."

She gulped, seeing the tenderness in his eyes. She didn't know what to say.

Joash eyes registered pain, and he looked as if he were badly wounded. "And I'm sorry about our son, too. I can't blame you for being angry with me. I've done so many things that I'm sure you'll never be able to forgive me for." He choked on his next words. "Our son might be alive, if it weren't for my actions. I should never have yelled at you like I did, or distrusted you."

Keturah blinked. He blamed himself for their son's death? And he thought she was angry with him for it? How much had he carried with him since that day? Why did he never say so?

Oh, Keturah, moaned inwardly. She'd been mistaken, about everything. If the things he was saying were true, she'd judged him so wrongly.

She noticed the injured look in his eyes and realized how beaten and undone he was. It wasn't in his nature to lose, but it was obvious to her that he'd accepted defeat.

Something struck deep inside her at the torn look in his eyes. When she realized he meant what he said, she suddenly wanted to go to him and offer him comfort.

He got up and went to his horse, taking the reigns. "Come." He gestured to her. "I'll take you back, if it's what you want. You can even go to Shiloh and your family. I've no hold over you anymore." He turned to her, wiping the wetness from his face.

She gulped, an incredulous look on her face. She could barely speak, knowing he was willing to let her go back to her family. She never imagined he would do such a thing. "To Shiloh?"

He nodded, letting out a slow breath, and looking away.

Her eyes were a mixture of sadness and understanding. She didn't move when he gestured to her again. "You never told me this. You didn't say."

He turned, watching her. "Keturah?"

A New Dance

"You never told me you prayed." She stared at him. "Why didn't you tell me any of this?"

There was a small measure of hope in his eyes when he looked back at her. "I thought you knew. I thought you could see it."

"But, I didn't." Her eyes were wide. "I thought..."

Joash started toward her.

"No." She put out her hand. "I have to think. And there's something I have to say."

He looked impatient, but stood back and listened.

She untied the pouch, hanging from the tie on her waist and took out the glittering stone he'd given her. He looked surprised that she had it there.

She turned it in her hand. "You can't see how beautiful it is, unless you look really hard in this light. But, it's there."

He moved toward her, but she cautioned him to stay where he was. "I didn't see what I should have." Her cheeks were flushed. "I thought you were angry with *me* for losing our son. And that you only wanted the child."

A tear formed in the corner of her eye, and she pushed it back. "I'm sorry."

Joash reached up and touched the side of her face. "I want children with you, Keturah. And maybe that's what my first intentions were, without the love. But now, whether we have them or not, matters little to me."

She drew in a breath, her eyes wide. She stared at him as if not knowing what to say at first.

Her voice grew soft. "When you took me from my home and family, you told me something. You said, that when the dancing ended, that I needed to leave everything else I also loved in the past."

Joash looked pained. "But, I was wrong. I said so many things I can't take back. I'm sorry for this, too. It's true that the Lord's changed me. I'm different now."

She sighed. "I wish I'd known this."

He reached out and touched the braid that had slipped over her shoulder.

She eyed him sadly. "The consequences of sin are deep, but so is the Lord's love, and he can redeem our sin. I was taken from my family and my home. But, now you're my home. And you're my family."

A tear slipped down her cheek. "And I can forgive you for the past."

There was tenderness in his eyes when he looked at her.

She sighed, sad that she hadn't realized his feelings before, so wrapped up she'd been in her own grief. A love she'd never known she was capable of suddenly struck her, and she wanted him to know it. She moved around the fire.

When he tried to go to her, she held up her hand. "I've something to show you, first." She motioned for him to take a seat by the fire.

He let out an impatient breath and sat down, not taking his eyes from her.

She took off her scarf from around her shoulders and laid it on the ground and untied her sandals, tossing them to the side, and stood in front of the fire barefoot. Then, she took the leather ties that bound her braid together and loosened them and let her hair fall freely over her shoulders.

Joash eyes were trained on her every move. He seemed mesmerized, and a smile widened on his face.

"I've begun a new dance." And then she smiled. "One for the husband I love."

***

Joash felt something stir in him he'd never known possible as he watched Keturah turn in the firelight on the mountain, under the full moon. She moved with the grace of a deer, to the rhythm of the night sounds, lifting her face to the stars, and then back to him, her eyes sparkling. Her dark, loose hair fell in thick waves against her back, and a song in her heart whispered to him through her gentle movements.

He took his eyes from her for a moment and looked up to the stars, realizing all his prayers had been answered in the Lord's time. The Lord had turned his sorrow to joy and his mourning into dancing. As his forefather Abraham, when he laid the one he loved most on the sacrificial altar, his Lord answered. And it was good. Better than he could ever wish for.

He gave thanks to the One who had the power to redeem his sin and free him from the man he used to be.

A New Dance

***

When Keturah finished dancing, Joash went to her and took her in his arms. He leaned down and kissed her, with a passion she'd not known. And she realized in that moment, she'd finally found a home that could replace Shiloh. The Lord had made it possible.

***

When Joash took Keturah from the horse in front of the courtyard the next morning, Simeon came stomping out of the gate. "Joash, you've gone too far this time!"

Nissa and her mother followed, giving him admonishing looks.

Joash started to laugh and looked at Keturah with an amused expression.

"Oh, my dear girl." Mary crooned, as she came toward them. She looked at her son with pursed lips and reached out to take Keturah's arm.

Nissa moved forward.

But, Keturah put up her hand. "No, wait."

She stood in front of Joash, who wrapped his arm around her waist and leaned down to kiss her neck.

"And you, too." She chided him, pulling away, but taking his hand in hers and looking up at him with rosy cheeks.

She turned back to the other's surprised expressions. "Joash was right. He finally decided to listen to the Lord. It seems even the most difficult sort can be redeemed."

Mary, Simeon and Nissa all stared at them in wonder, their faces breaking into smiles.

No one spoke, but just eyed them both curiously, as Joash shot her a sideways glance and lifted her into his arms carrying her past them to the house, leaving them standing at the gate with their mouths open.

Joash put Keturah down on the other side of the doorway. He grinned as he leaned down to kiss her again.

The color in her cheeks deepened, but she held tight to him.

He smiled. "What would you say if I told you, I'd like to take you to visit Shiloh again, and see your family? I want to know if they still have that little goat of yours, Betsalel, so I can get him for you."

She let out a breath, her eyes full of wonder. "Shiloh?"

He grinned and nodded.

"And bring back Betsalel?"

He laughed. "Yes. I'll get him for you and anything else you want."

She threw her arms around him and held tight to him. "Oh!"

Keturah's heart swelled with the great things the Lord had done. All her prayers had been answered, not in the way she imagined, but in the Lord's way and in his time.

So many times she had wondered why the Lord hadn't seemed to listen, but on this day she realized he had. It was only that she didn't see the answer to her prayers until now.

Maybe, it was like Tirzah said, that she wouldn't see every one of the Lord's promises right away, but sometimes had to wait in faith, like many others had before her.

She took Joash's arm in hers and smiled. How wonderful that her wait for her husband was over and that the Lord blessed her with a good man, despite the difficulties she faced getting there.

"I'll never forget this day." She stood looking up at Joash.

Joash stopped and lifted his hand to her face, stroking it gently. "God is good. He is able. We only have to believe in him."

"Yes, this is true. With faith, anything is possible."

***

Judges 21:20-25, King James Version

20 "So they instructed the Benjamites, saying, "Go and hide in the vineyards **21** and watch. When the young women of Shiloh come out to join in the dancing, rush from the vineyards and each of you seize one of them to be your wife. Then return to the land of Benjamin. **22** When their fathers or brothers complain to us, we will say to them, 'Do us the favor of helping them, because we did not get wives for them during the war. You will not be guilty of breaking your oath because you did not give your daughters to them.'" **23** So that is what the Benjamites did. While the young women were dancing, each man caught one and carried her off to be his wife. Then they returned to their inheritance and rebuilt the towns and settled in them. **24** At that time the Israelites left that place and went home to their tribes and clans, each to his own inheritance. **25** In those days Israel had no king; **everyone did as they saw fit.**"

Those in Old Testament times relied on faith in God. And yet, we also can trust God's son, Jesus, to save us. The following verses explain how we can know for sure we can have eternal life with him.

"For all have sinned, and come short of the glory of God;" Romans 3:23 (King James's Version)

"For the wages of sin is death; but the gift of God is eternal life through Jesus Christ our Lord." Romans 6:23 (King James's Version) "But God commendeth his love toward us, in that, while we were yet sinners, Christ died for us." Romans 5:8 (King James's Version)

"That if thou shalt confess with thy mouth the Lord Jesus, and shalt believe in thine heart that God hath raised him from the dead, thou shalt be saved." Romans 10:9 (King James's Version)

These things have I written unto you that believe on the name of the Son of God; that ye may know that ye have eternal life, and that ye may believe on the name of the Son of God. 1 John 5:13 (King James's Version)

*All quotes taken from the King James's Version of the Holy Scripture.

Made in the USA
Charleston, SC
08 October 2015